"I can be very stubborn,"
she told him angrily

"Mulish, don't you mean?" Roberto flashed her a mocking grin. "But I'm very good at overcoming any sort of resistance."

"Why are you doing this?" she whispered.

"Because you ran away from me. You preferred to be engaged to Aubrey rather than live with me. You even preferred your silly job to living with me."

"It isn't a silly job," Norma retorted.

"Your engagement is nothing but a defense," he went on angrily as if she hadn't spoken. "With a little luck you'll lose both Aubrey and your job after tonight." He gave her a wicked glance. "And then you'll not be so quick to reject any proposition I might make to you. You might even jump at the chance to be my mistress."

Books by Flora Kidd

HARLEQUIN PRESENTS

400—WIFE BY CONTRACT
434—BEYOND CONTROL
447—PERSONAL AFFAIR
464—PASSIONATE STRANGER
485—BRIDE FOR A CAPTAIN
495—MEETING AT MIDNIGHT
520—MAKEBELIEVE MARRIAGE
554—BETWEEN PRIDE AND PASSION
577—TEMPTED TO LOVE
592—DARK SEDUCTION
643—TROPICAL TEMPEST
657—DANGEROUS ENCOUNTER
682—PASSIONATE PURSUIT
729—DESPERATE DESIRE
756—THE OPEN MARRIAGE
771—FLIGHT TO PASSION
834—A SECRET PLEASURE

HARLEQUIN ROMANCE

1865—STRANGER IN THE GLEN
1907—ENCHANTMENT IN BLUE
1977—THE DANCE OF COURTSHIP
1999—THE SUMMER WIFE
2056—THE BLACK KNIGHT
2146—TO PLAY WITH FIRE
2228—THE BARGAIN BRIDE

These books may be available at your local bookseller.

Don't miss any of our special offers. Write to us at the following address for information on our newest releases.

Harlequin Reader Service
P.O. Box 52040, Phoenix, AZ 85072-2040
Canadian address: P.O. Box 2800, Postal Station A,
5170 Yonge St., Willowdale, Ont. M2N 6J3

FLORA KIDD

a secret pleasure

Harlequin Books

TORONTO • NEW YORK • LONDON
AMSTERDAM • PARIS • SYDNEY • HAMBURG
STOCKHOLM • ATHENS • TOKYO • MILAN

Harlequin Presents first edition November 1985
ISBN 0-373-10834-6

Original hardcover edition published in 1985
by Mills & Boon Limited

CHAPTER ONE

WHEN he heard that she was going to Italy on business for the public relations company that employed her, Norma Seton's stepfather Roy Elton invited her to have dinner with him at the old house he lived in in Barnes, just up the river Thames from Putney.

'What exactly are you going to do?' he asked when they were both settled in large armchairs in his comfortable study and were sipping sherry. Since it was the beginning of November it was already dark at six-thirty, but he hadn't drawn the heavy brocade curtains and from her chair Norma could see the fine tracery of leafless branches etched against a light streak in the western sky.

'Rome first, for a day and two nights, then by train to Florence where we'll spend two nights and a day too. Then we have two days off, so we thought we'd go to Venice by train and stay an afternoon and a night there before going by bus to Milan for another two nights and a day,' she replied.

Slim and straight in green velvet breeches, knee-high leather boots and a shiny white blouse with full bishop sleeves, her bright auburn hair cut short and falling in casual fronds over her forehead, Norma looked more like a pageboy from some medieval court of love than she did a contemporary young woman with very decided

views on feminism, thought Roy, observing her
affectionately. Fairly easygoing himself and
rather absentminded, absorbed in his work as a
Professor of English Literature at a London
university, he was always amazed by Norma's
brisk business ability and her powers of organisa-
tion. He thought she was highly suited for the
career in public relations that she had decided to
follow when she had graduated from university
with a degree in Business Administration.

'And what will you be doing while you're over
there?' he asked.

'Oh, looking at various hotels and deciding
which one is the most suitable to hold a book-
launching luncheon in,' she replied. 'Brenton &
Humbolt have hired us to organise a promotional
in Rome, Florence and Milan to launch the
translations of their best-seller suspense-thriller
line into Italian. Jeremy Jenson, their top
novelist, will be at all three of the luncheons and
will sign books. I have to make sure there'll be
media coverage for the luncheons and that
invitations go out to all the right people, and that
all the small details are attended to, like flowers
for the tables and so on. I got the job because I'm
the only one at Bright & Stevens who can speak
Italian with any fluency, thanks to Mama's
teaching.'

'And not because you have an "in" with
Aubrey Brenton, chief executive of Brenton &
Humbolt?' remarked Roy with a grin.

'Well, Aubrey might have had something to do
with it,' she admitted, grinning back at him.

'Do you know anyone in Rome?'

'No. But Melinda Morrison, Brenton &

Humbolt's public relations director, will be with me, so I'll have company.'

'Aubrey isn't going?'

'No. He's in Germany at the moment and he won't be back before I leave. I won't be seeing him until I return from Milan.' Norma sipped some sherry, gave him a glance from under her lashes and added rather diffidently, 'He's asked me to marry him.'

'Really? Well, I suppose it's about time, and I'm not really surprised. You and he have been friendly for over three years now. In fact I'm surprised you haven't shacked up together before now.'

'Oh, Roy!' Norma's laughter made her golden-brown eyes dance and her white teeth glint. 'Can you really imagine Aubrey shacking up with a woman? I can't. He's terribly conventional, you know—likes to do all the right things. Anyway, even if he had asked me to shack up, as you call it, I couldn't have agreed. I could only live with a man who paid me the compliment of asking me to marry him. That's something else I learned from Mama. There has to be commitment from both sides before a relationship can work or grow.'

'True enough,' remarked Roy. 'Have you accepted his proposal? Are you going to marry him?'

'I haven't made up my mind yet. I told him I'd think about it while I was away in Italy and let him know when we meet again.'

'I see. You're being very cautious.'

'Well, marriage is a big step for me to take. I enjoy being single and I want to continue with my career. What do you think? Do you think Aubrey and I are well matched?'

'No,' he replied honestly. 'You need a man who'll master you.'

'Oh, Roy, you are funny!' She laughed again. 'In this day and age? Have you forgotten women are liberated now? They've liberated themselves from male domination. Besides, that's why I like Aubrey. He doesn't try to dominate me. And he's a good companion. We like the same things—the same music, the same books, the same sports activities.'

'And what about love? Do you love one another?'

'You mean do we feel passionate about each other?'

'That's one way of putting it.'

'Well, we've made mild love a few times, when we've gone out together,' she admitted reluctantly.

'That isn't exactly what I mean by passion,' said Roy. 'I mean, do you feel unhappy when you're apart from each other. Do you *yearn* to be together?'

'Not really. Our relationship is much more . . . much more. . .' Norma paused, searching for the right word.

'Cerebral?' he suggested mockingly. 'More to do with the mind than with the heart?'

'Yes. I was going to say platonic.'

'Good God, Norma!' he exclaimed. 'A platonic friendship is hardly a good reason for marriage!'

'Why not?'

'There has to be more than just communicating with each other on a mental or spiritual level. There has to be some gut feeling. Here,' he punched himself low down, 'in the stomach.' He gave her a narrowed searching glance. 'I don't believe you've ever been in love. Oh, I know you had some boy-and-girl affairs in your late teens, but you've never been really and truly in love, have you?'

'I . . . I. . . .'

'You wouldn't hesitate to answer my question if you had. You'd know about it if you had. You'd know about love's sweet anguish, its tender magic, its wild rapture. And you're not in love with Aubrey, so you shouldn't marry him.'

'Oh, dear!' she grumbled. 'Now I wish I hadn't asked for your opinion. You've made me feel more mixed up than ever. Can we change the subject?'

'Of course. I'd much prefer to talk to you about Rome and Florence, tell you of places you should visit if you have time—and that brings me to my reason for inviting you here this evening. When you're in Rome I'd like you to find someone for me and give him something.'

Roy went over to the desk and took something out of a drawer. With a package in his hand, he came back to his chair.

'What is it?' asked Norma. The package was wrapped in clear plastic and was tied with a red ribbon.

'Letters. Love letters—six of them. All written to your mother during the period she lived in Rome after your father was killed and she took lessons from the Italian tenor Roberto Cortelli. I was looking through her diaries and I came across this package that was with them. You'll see there's a note with them, signed by her.'

Norma took the package from him, thinking of

her mother, the beautiful and stately Maria Crossley, half English and half Italian, who had died so tragically at the height of her career as an opera singer only two months ago after a fight with throat cancer. Although she hadn't seen much of her mother over the years, because Maria had spent at least eight months of every year 'on the road' travelling from country to country to sing in operatic performances, Norma had adored her. Everyone had.

Under the ribbon that tied the package was a piece of Maria's notepaper with the initials M. C. entwined and embossed on it in the left upper corner. Even though she had been married twice, first to Norma's father Alan Seton, who had been killed in a motor-cycle crash soon after Norma's birth, leaving his eighteen-year-old wife and tiny daughter almost destitute, and then later to Roy Elton, Maria had never changed her last name and had always appeared professionally as Maria Crossley.

On the piece of paper was written:

'Please return these letters to Roberto Cortelli when I die. His address in Rome is on one of the letters. I promised I would return them to him.'

The date on the note was August, a month before Maria's death.

'Do you know this man Cortelli?' Norma asked Roy.

'I know of him, but I've never met him.' Roy's lips curved in a wry smile and he ruffled his already rumpled greying brown hair. 'Going by the letters, she and Cortelli had quite an affair going while she was taking singing lessons from him.'

'You've read the letters, then.'

'I have. They're very passionate and poetical. Written in pretty good English too, which surprises me. Although he probably had to sing in English sometimes and had learned to speak a rough sort of pidgin English I can hardly believe Roberto Cortelli could have been capable of writing the literary English used in those letters.'

'Didn't Mama ever tell you she'd had an affair with him?' asked Norma.

'No, she didn't. Oh, I was aware that there'd been someone in Rome who had taken her fancy for a while. But we didn't discuss our past love affairs with each other. We both felt that anything like that, that had happened before we had met each other, had nothing to do with our love and friendship for each other. All that mattered was the love between us, and since we both took our marriage vows seriously we were both determined to remain faithful to each other in thought and deed even though we knew we would spend much time apart while pursuing our separate careers.'

'I know what you mean,' Norma nodded. 'That's the sort of marriage I hope I shall have.' She looked down at the package. 'Are you sure Roberto Cortelli is still alive?'

'No, I'm not. He was quite a lot older than Maria and he must be over seventy now. The address, by the way, is Via Scipione. I looked it up on a street map I have of Rome. It's on the Vatican side of the river Tiber.'

'Why don't you post the letters to him?'

'I had thought of doing that, but I'm not sure he's still living there and I wouldn't like them to

be lost. I was going to write to him to find out if
he was still at that address, but when you told me
you'd be going to Rome next Sunday I thought
you wouldn't mind checking out if he's still there,
and if he is, you could give the letters to him.
Will you do that? Will you carry out your
mother's final instructions concerning the letters?'

'Of course I will. But if he isn't there what
then?'

'Find out from whoever lives in the house
where he's living now and send them to him.'

'And if I find out that he's no longer living?'

'Bring the letters back to me, please, and I'll
put them with her diaries for the day when I
intend to start going through them for information for the biography I intend to write of her. I
might want to use the letters, or at least refer to
them and quote from them.'

'May I read them?' asked Norma.

'If you want to.' Again Roy ruffled his hair,
then stroked his beard, his faded blue eyes gazing
off into the distance. 'I have to admit they puzzle
me,' he said. 'They don't quite fit in with the
image I have of Cortelli as a middle-aged opera
singer who had retired from performance in order
to teach because he was tired of traipsing round
the world. The letters seem very youthful to me.
They read as if they'd been written by a young
man in the first throes of romantic love and I
use the word romantic in its proper sense.
These are outpourings by a man who worships a
woman who's unattainable, rather like the
outpourings of passion by the English Romantic
poets; you know, Keats, Shelley, Byron. In fact

there are many direct quotes from their poems and other English poets. Anyway, you read them and see what you think.' He gave her a keen glance. 'I hope you don't mind finding out that your mother possibly had a love affair with Cortelli without being married to him.'

'Who am I to cast stones at my own mother?' she replied. 'I know that she loved my father and I know that she loved you truly. She always came back to you, she once told me, because she loved you very much and felt comfortable with you. I'm sure any affair she had with Cortelli was a slight aberration on her part. It probably wouldn't have happened if she'd met you before she went to Rome to have lessons from him.'

'Yes, she always came back to me,' murmured Roy sadly. 'Ours was a very good and very satisfying marriage and love affair. I miss her.'

'I know you do. I do too,' Norma told him. 'I wish. . .' She broke off, thinking of Aubrey and how unpassionate their friendship was.

'You wish what?'

'Oh, I was just going to say I wish she hadn't died,' sighed Norma. 'I really could do with her advice right now.'

'About Aubrey, you mean?' Roy guessed shrewdly, and she nodded.

'She would tell you to follow your heart and not your head. That was always her philosophy,' said Roy, and stood up. 'Now come into the kitchen and supervise my cooking. I'm trying to make *moo-goo-gai-pan*. Know anything about Chinese cooking?'

The following Sunday morning Norma flew to

Rome and went by taxi from the airport to the hotel on the Via Veneto where she was booked in for two nights. She intended to spend the afternoon getting her bearings and having a look at the city and the evening preparing for the hectic round of appointments she had to keep with various people on Monday.

After lunching on lasagna such as she had never eaten before, the pasta and meat filling melting in her mouth, she decided to take advantage of the warm autumn afternoon to walk in the Villa Borghese park which she had discovered she could reach easily from her hotel by walking up the Via Veneto to the Piazza Brasile.

The sun shone down out of a hazy blue sky and all Rome seemed to be taking the air in the extensive park. Old buildings glowed golden-brown. Huge Roman pine trees, shaped like inside-out umbrellas, seemed to sweep the sky with their feathery tops. The reddish leaves of oak trees and the bronze-coloured leaves of plane trees crunched under her feet.

In the Galoppatoio riders were cantering their horses. Young men with black hair, dressed in the inevitable blue jeans, played soccer in a wide green field. Dogs walked with their owners and many children skipped and shouted, out for the afternoon with their sedately strolling parents. Kites sailed, flashes of bright colour against the blue.

Along a pathway lined with magnolia trees Norma wandered into another park, and after buying an ice cream from a stall selling not only ice-cream but canned soft drinks, huge sugary doughnuts and smoked meat sandwiches, she leaned with many other young people against a stone balustrade that looked out over a *piazza* busy with cars and buses that had a tall stone obelisk in its centre, a reminder of how ancient the city was. Across the square her gaze lifted to the tiled roofs of many tall old buildings and beyond them to the magical basilica of St Peter's, its huge dome glittering in the sunlight, higher than anything else.

She looked at her street map. The square she could see below was the Piazza del Popolo. From there it wasn't far to the river and a bridge called Regina Margherita. If she crossed the bridge and turned right along an avenue beside the river she would eventually come to the Via Scipione.

Should she go now, take a chance on Roberto Cortelli being at home? She would have to try and contact him today because tomorrow she would be too busy. She glanced at her watch. Almost three o'clock. It wouldn't take her long to walk to the Via Scipione and she had the letters with her, in her shoulder bag. They had been there since she had read them on the flight over the Alps to Italy that morning, and having read them she was now eager to meet the man who had written them to her mother, the man who had been so romantically and passionately in love with his much younger singing pupil.

She supposed she should make sure he lived on the Via Scipione still. She would go down to the square and find a telephone booth and look in the directory. If there wasn't a directory then she would take a chance and walk over to the house.

The way down to the square was two flights of

wide stone steps, and she soon found a phone booth on an island in the middle of the square where people waited for buses and women sold flowers from baskets. Fortunately there was a directory chained to the phone booth, and there weren't many Cortellis in it. The name Roberto Cortelli seemed to leap up at her from the page. He still lived in a house on the Via Scipione.

She soon discovered how to use the phone and within a few minutes was listening to another phone ringing at the end of the line. A man's voice, deep and pleasant, answered at last.

'I would like to speak to Signor Roberto Cortelli, please,' she said in slow, careful but correct Italian.

There was a short pause, then the voice, which now held an undercurrent of amusement, said in English that was crisped by a slight American accent,

'This is Roberto Cortelli speaking.'

'Oh!' Norma was surprised. 'How do you know I'm English?' she exclaimed.

'By your accent when you speak Italian,' he replied, sounding even more amused.

'But I speak good Italian,' she retorted.

'Your phrasing is good, but you speak with an accent and your voice drops at the end of phrases and sentences,' he replied. 'That is English. Who are you?'

'I'm Norma Seton. You don't know me, but I believe you used to know my mother, Maria Crossley, the opera singer.'

Another silence. She could hear him breathing at the other end of the line. Was it possible he had forgotten her mother? Sometimes elderly people did lose their memories of people they had known quite intimately at one time. Often they forgot names. She was just going to speak again, to remind him that he used to teach her mother singing, when he spoke,

'Yes, I used to know Maria. I read in a newspaper that she had died in September. I'm sorry to know that. If I had known where she lived I would have sent flowers, or even come to her funeral,' he said. His voice didn't sound old; it sounded warm and vigorous. But then voices could be deceptive over the phone. 'You have my sympathy in your great loss,' he added softly. 'Maria was a very wonderful person.'

'Thank you,' she whispered. He sounded really upset now. 'When she died she left instructions for a package to be sent to you, and when my stepfather learned that I was coming to Rome on business he asked me to look you up and to give the package to you. I was wondering if I could bring it to you this afternoon. I'm not far from where you live and I could be at your house in half an hour. Would that be convenient?'

He was silent again. She waited. He said at last, 'How long are you staying in Rome?'

'I leave on Tuesday morning for Florence, but I'll be busy all tomorrow.'

'Then please come now. I have to go out later. Do you know how to get here?'

'Yes, I think so.'

'Then I look forward to meeting you in half an hour,' he said, and hung up.

Leaving the telephone booth, Norma made her way to the Regina Margherita bridge. Traffic, made up mostly of small box-like Fiats, surged along beside her over the bridge. She looked over the white stone parapet that edged the roadway. Below, the Tiber seemed to ooze along rather than flow, a green sluggish stream, low at this time of the year. When she had crossed the bridge she turned right and walked along beside the river under the branches of many big plane trees, enjoying the crunching of leaves beneath her boots.   –

The Via Scipione, which was at right angles to the avenue and the river, was a pleasant tree-lined street of big stone villas that stood back from the roadway behind high walls. Walking along the pavement was difficult because so many cars were parked with their front wheels on it. Norma had to dodge in and out of them until she reached the Cortelli house.

It was also behind high walls and there was an elegant wrought iron gate. Through the bars of the gate she could see a courtyard where geraniums, begonias and roses were still flowering among luxuriant green shrubs. The house was ginger-coloured and square. Behind its roof parapet she could see a small dome of glass glittering in the sunshine. Outside the upper windows was a balcony over the railings of which trailing plants were festooned. Under the balcony were two long windows and a doorway with a semi-circular fanlight above it.

She tried to push open the gate and found that it was locked. In the wall on the right side of the gate was a bell-push with the number of the house above it. She pressed the bell-push. After a while the front door opened and a man in dark trousers and white jacket appeared and came slowly down the steps and along the pathway to the gate. She wondered if he was Roberto Cortelli, but when he came closer she decided he couldn't be. Through the bars of the gate he stared at her with suspicious black eyes that were set in a low-browed broad-cheeked swarthy face. His black hair was plentifully sprinkled with grey.

'I have come to see Signor Cortelli,' said Norma in Italian. 'I have just talked to him on the phone. He is expecting me.'

He inclined his head slightly in acknowledgment, and unlocked the gate with a key from a ring of keys that was attached to his waist by a chain, then he indicated that she should step into the courtyard. She slid past him and he locked the gate. She followed him along the pathway, up the steps and into the house.

The entrance hall was wide and high. It had a mosaic floor, tiny stones of different colours laid down in a geometric design. The walls were covered with faded gold and green striped wallpaper and against them hung several large paintings that looked like originals. At one side a staircase, uncarpeted, each tread and riser made from gleaming golden-brown wood, led up to a gallery with wrought iron railings that ran round three of the walls. Sunlight shone in through the glass dome in the roof that she had seen from the road.

The man, who she guessed was a servant of some sort, led her between two graceful marble pillars of Corinthian design into a long room that had windows at both ends. The window at the back of the house was French and was slightly open, revealing a patio garden outside with high walls around it. Thin carpet, slightly threadbare in places, covered the floor. Once it had been thick and luxurious, she suspected, and had come from Persia, judging by its dark blues and reds. Against the walls two sofas were arranged, both covered in gold and beige brocade that had lost its pattern in some places. There were also armchairs covered in the same brocade, a few occasional tables and an antique desk set under the front window. A splendid crystal chandelier hung from the centre of the ceiling that was decorated with intricate plaster mouldings.

The servant suggested that she should sit down and then went away. Norma didn't sit but wandered about the room admiring the antique furniture, intrigued by the house and wondering how old it was. She looked out of the French window. In the centre of the walled garden was a statue of a boy, cast in bronze. He was holding a bowl on one shoulder. From the bowl water trickled out into another larger bowl in which the boy was standing. Around this fountain was a circle of stone flags laid flat on the ground. On the flags white-painted wrought iron garden furniture was scattered about, looking as if the people who had been sitting on it had only just left. Small trees—she thought some of them looked like almond and orange trees—grew in the shelter of the walls and there were many shrubs and rose bushes.

Returning to the room, she wandered over to the huge fireplace. Built of stone, it was of ancient design and the hearth was big enough to sit in. There was a dog-grate filled with logs.

Above the shelf of the fireplace, on the wall, hung a small tapestry. Its colours faded, it seemed to depict a knight on horseback with a lance in his hand. At his feet writhed a dragon. Norma wondered if the knight was St George and looked for the damsel he was supposed to have rescued from the monster. She was just leaning closer trying to make out some lettering at the bottom of the tapestry when the voice that had spoken to her on the phone spoke behind her with sharp authority.

'Don't touch it—it's very fragile.'

She stepped back quickly and almost guiltily and swung around to face the man who had come into the room. Her eyes opened wide in surprise when she saw how different he was from what she had expected.

Instead of the elderly man with thin possibly snow-white hair, a slightly bent lean figure, possibly leaning on a stick, whom she had expected to see, she saw a tall man in his prime whose straight black hair sprang back from his high forehead to wave behind his ears. He stood straight, his wide shoulders set proudly, his long muscular legs slightly apart and shaping the close-fitting dark pants he was wearing. He was wearing an elegant yet casual bombardier jacket that she guessed had been styled by Armani and was made from smooth grey suede. The jacket was unzipped as if he had just put it on and under it was wearing a thin multi-coloured round-necked sweater.

Standing totally still, he surveyed her with long dark eyes set above high prominent cheekbones, taking in her high-necked white blouse, tweed hacking jacket, longish full black woollen skirt and short leather boots with turned-down tops. His stare was disconcerting and gave her the feeling that he knew much more about her than she knew about him. It also made her feel guiltier than ever about having been caught staring at the tapestry, and that annoyed her. After all, she'd had no intention of touching it, so she sprang quickly to her own defence.

'I wasn't going to touch it. I was just looking at it trying to make out the letters at the bottom. I thought it might be a Gobelin,' she said with a touch of defiance.

CHAPTER TWO

HE seemed to become aware that he had been staring at her too long and moved towards her with graceful long-legged strides to stand beside her and look up at the tapestry.

'It is a Gobelin,' he said. 'And like everything else in this house it is very old and on the verge of disintegration. Except this fireplace.' He slapped the stone shelf of the fireplace with one hand. 'This is sixteenth century and the Sicilian *contessa* who had this house built for her at the end of the eighteenth century had it moved stone by stone from her castle outside Palermo.' He turned to her and smiled, holding out his right hand.

'I'm Roberto Cortelli,' he said. 'You of course are Norma, Maria's daughter. I'm pleased to meet you at last. Welcome to Rome.'

Both his smile and his announcement that he was indeed Roberto Cortelli astonished Norma, and for a few seconds she could only stare at him, tongue-tied for once, while she struggled with a feeling that was new to her; a feeling of overwhelming attraction towards him. Never had any man had this effect on her. Still staring at him, she shook his hand. His grasp was warm and hard, and now that she was close to him she could see his eyes were a dark grey, the colour of a stormy sea, and they continued to look at her steadily and appraisingly as if he were searching for some resemblance to Maria in her face.

'But you're too young!' she blurted out at last. If, as she guessed, he was about thirty-five or six, he could have been only a teenager when her mother had stayed in this house about nineteen years ago, too young to have been Maria's lover.

'Too young for what?' he demanded, frowning at her, the smile gone, leaving his face looking hard and severe.

'To be the Roberto Cortelli my mother used to know and who gave her singing lessons. Too young to have been her teacher,' she explained. 'Roy Elton, my stepfather, said he thought Cortelli would be over seventy by now.'

'He was referring, I guess, to my father,' he replied. 'And you're quite right—I couldn't have given your mother singing lessons. But he did.'

'Then where is he?'

'Unfortunately he also died earlier this year, in August, just before Maria died.'

'Oh—I'm sorry. I don't think she knew. She was very ill at the end, in great pain, and she didn't really know what was going on in the world. Roy didn't know your father had died either. He wouldn't have asked me to bring the package of letters to him if he had. Oh, I wish you'd told me that he'd died when I phoned you earlier!'

He frowned again and gave her a puzzled glance.

'But you didn't ask me about him,' he pointed out. 'You said only that you believed I used to know your mother. And I did know Maria. We were very good friends.'

'But if I'd known your father had died I wouldn't have bothered to come here this afternoon,' Norma complained. She was fast becoming aware that the walk across two parks and over the river in her boots had raised blisters on both of her heels.

'Do you know what is in the package?' he asked.

'Letters. There are six of them, and they were all written to my mother when she studied with him here in Rome.'

'Do you have the package with you? I'd like to see the letters,' he said autocratically.

His height, the width of his shoulders, his intent dark grey stare were dominating. There was an arrogance about him that rubbed her the wrong way. Dark and somehow ruthless with his wickedly slanting narrow eyes and his handsome chiselled features, he was a challenge to her femininity. She sensed that he was accustomed to getting his own way where women were concerned, and if he couldn't charm a woman into giving him what he wanted he would take it anyway. Straightening her shoulders, refusing to be dominated, she lifted her head, tilted her chin and stared back at him.

'Why do you want to see them?' she asked.

'To make sure my father wrote them, of course.'

'He did. He signed them all with his full name, Roberto Cortelli.'

'How do you know he signed them? Have you ever seen his handwriting?' he queried coolly. 'Did you ever meet him and see him write his name?'

'Er ... no, I didn't.' She was momentarily defeated by his smooth argument but recovered quickly and came back with, 'But there is a note on them written by my mother giving instructions that they should be returned to him if she died—look!'

She took the package out of her shoulder bag and held it out, pointing to the note. He looked at the note and read the message on it.

'It says only that the package should be returned to Roberto Cortelli,' he commented, not looking at her.

'And it gives the date ... just a few days before she died. She must have had a few moments of consciousness when she remembered them and found them and wrote the note. At least, that's what Roy suspects must have happened. You see, she did spend the last few weeks at home in her own room with a private nurse to look after her,' Norma explained.

He went on looking at the note, and then suddenly he snatched the package from her hand and turning his back to her slid the ribbon off so that the note written by her mother fluttered to the floor.

'Oh! Give them back to me!' demanded Norma angrily, annoyed that he had taken them without her being able to stop him. He took no notice of her demand, so picking up the note from the floor she went round to face him, reaching a hand out to take the package from him. He raised a hand and knocked her hand away, then strode past her to the antique desk. By the time she reached his side he had unlocked a drawer in the desk and was putting the letters in it.

'Give them back to me!' Norma demanded again, stretching a hand out to the drawer.

'No.' Again he struck her hand away, slammed the drawer shut and locked it with a key on a ring of keys that he shoved into his trouser pocket.

Hands in both trouser pockets, he turned to her. She glared up at him, wanting to berate him for what he had done, to accuse him of being an overbearing thief and to demand that he give the letters back to her—but for some reason words failed her when he looked at her with a slight smile curling his lips and his eyes dancing with a secret kind of laughter.

'I'd like to keep them for a while,' he said eventually. 'I want to look at them and read them and make sure they were written by my father. I think that's a fairly reasonable request.'

'But . . . but . . . I'm not even sure you are his son,' argued Norma. 'How do I know you're really the person you say you are?'

The impact of his powerful personality was having a very strange effect on her. Antagonism was fading fast before his cool quick actions and reasonable arguments. He gave the impression of being a man who knew his own mind, made decisions quickly and acted upon them while completely ignoring any opposition.

'I can easily supply you with identification,' he replied imperturbably. 'Paolo, who let you into the house, has run the house here for more than twenty years. First he served my father. Now he keeps house for me—although like most of the furniture in this house his joints are disintegrating and he is likely to fall to pieces at any moment. For all that, he's a loyal worker and he can vouch for who I am. He'll tell you I'm really the person I say I am, the son of the Roberto Cortelli who used to teach singing. He might even remember Maria, if you ask him. Shall I call him in?'

'No, no, it doesn't matter.' She was defeated again by his good humour. 'I believe you're Roberto Cortelli. But I still don't like the way you stole the letters from me.'

'You don't look much like Maria,' he said, coming closer to her. 'Only about the eyes are you like her. Amber eyes with dark centres. Tiger eyes, *"burning bright, in the forests of the night"*. Do your eyes blaze in the night? I'd like to find out. But unlike Maria's, your hair is flame-coloured.' He raised a hand and with one finger flicked the fronds that fell across her forehead as he might have flicked the hair of a young child. 'Maria used to talk about you,' he added. 'Her little girl whom she had left behind in England with her mother, your Italian grandmother, so that she could come here to improve her singing, learn to be a great opera singer. She once told me that your hair was the colour of a wild sunset.'

'My mother talked to you about me?' exclaimed Norma incredulously.

'Often, when we were in this house together and she was waiting for her lessons with my father.'

'But you could have only been sixteen or seventeen—only a schoolboy. Why would she talk to you?'

'Why wouldn't she?' he countered. 'In this country we mature early. By sixteen we are men and women, not boys and girls. The last year Maria was here I was eighteen—old enough to fall in love and to make love.'

He touched her cheek with long fingers, and tingles of alarm shot along her nerves, warning her that he was dangerous; warning her that if she let him kiss her she would never be the same. But she didn't step back, because from somewhere deep inside her came a desire to be kissed by him, to find out what it would be like.

His lips covered hers arrogantly in a sensual kiss that, at first, outraged her. The urge to slap his face sprang up in her, but as the kiss continued and his lips seduced hers to respond, the urge faded. Her lips parted on a sigh of pleasure and she gave herself up to the sensual delight of kissing him. His arms went around her. Her arms went around him and for a few moments they were locked together in an embrace, oblivious to everything but each other.

Then suddenly he was moving away from her, glancing at his watch.

'I regret I can't stay and talk with you any longer today,' he said. 'I have another appointment in fifteen minutes, so I must leave you. But we'll meet again before you go to Firenze. Tomorrow? For dinner? Which hotel are you staying in?'

Still bemused by his kiss, she told him the name of the hotel, then said,

'But I'm not sure I want to meet you again.'

'Don't you want the letters back?' he retorted with a wicked glint as he backed away from her on his way to the doorway. 'I'll bring them with me. I'll call for you at your hotel at a quarter to eight tomorrow evening. By then I'll have looked at the letters and will know whether my father wrote them or not. *Arrivederci*, Norma. Please excuse me. Paolo will show you out.'

'But . . . but . . . oh, damn!'

Finding she was talking to empty space, Norma stamped her foot. Then she hurried into the hallway. But Roberto had gone. Like a whirlwind he had come and gone, leaving her breathless, slightly dishevelled and thoroughly kissed, having robbed her of the letters. And now there was no opportunity for her to go back and force the desk drawer open and take the letters, because the old dark manservant had appeared.

'This way, *signorina*,' he said, and there was nothing else she could do but follow him out of the house, down the steps and along the path to the gate. As he unlocked the gate she experienced the eerie feeling that she was being watched and looked back at the house, up to the balcony. Was there someone standing at one of the upstairs windows watching her? Roberto?

She stepped through the open gateway. Paolo wished her good afternoon, then the gate clanged after her, the key grated in the lock. She walked away quickly along the leaf-strewn, car-strewn pavement without a backward glance.

Wishing she had thought to ask Roberto or Paolo to call a taxi for her, she walked all the way back to the Via Veneto. By the time she arrived at the hotel her blisters were worse and her head was aching from the effort of battling against the noise and flurry of Rome's ceaseless road traffic.

It was all the fault of Roberto Cortelli, she thought as she soaked in a bathtub of hot water. She should have had more sense and not gone to see him. She should have let him come to her.

But at the time of making the appointment to see him she had believed him to be an older man, commanding her respect and consideration and who, perhaps, wouldn't have found it easy to get about.

She pressed a hand against her lips. He had kissed her as if he had had the right to kiss her and had seemed to take her response for granted. He was probably accustomed to women submitting to his obviously expert lovemaking and had assumed she would submit too. And she had. She had! That was what was making her so angry. She didn't want to be taken for granted by him. She wanted to be the most important woman in his life, the woman he came back to, the woman he loved.

Heavens, what was she thinking of? She had met him only once and already she was wondering what it would be like to be loved by him! She was romancing about him. And that was strange, because she had never indulged in romantic fantasy before. She didn't spend time day-dreaming about Aubrey; in fact she hardly ever thought about him when she wasn't with him. Her friendship with him had so far been without passion, even though they had kissed many times. But Aubrey always kissed her as if it was something he was supposed to do and not because he wanted to.

The phone rang in the bedroom. Norma got out of the bath, wrapped a towel around her and went to answer it.

'Hello, Norma. Melinda here—Melinda Morrison, from Brenton & Humbolt,' said a rather drawling voice with a London accent. 'I've

just arrived. How would you like to meet me for
dinner in the hotel dining room at about seven-
thirty? We can discuss what we have to do
tomorrow.'

'That sounds great,' agreed Norma. Melinda
was Brenton & Humbolt's public relations
director and it was important that the woman
should be impressed and pleased by the person
Bright & Stevens had sent to assist her in Italy.
'I'll see you at seven-thirty.'

While she was dining Norma was able to forget
Roberto Cortelli, but he returned to her thoughts
later that night as she lay in bed trying to read
herself to sleep with one of Jeremy Jenson's
spine-chilling novels. Next day it was easy to
banish him again while she went around with
Melinda calling on all the people they had to see
regarding the forthcoming luncheon and translating back and forth.

They began their interviews with the manager
and chef of the hotel they were staying in and
were shown the ballroom and other facilities on
the mezzanine floor, where the manager told
them he would be pleased if they held the
luncheon there. Satisfied with the services the
hotel had to offer, Melinda booked the ballroom
for a date in February of the next year and also
the bedrooms for the party of people who would
be coming for the luncheon party from the
United Kingdom. Then they discussed the menu
for the luncheon with the chef. Afterwards they
set out to visit newspaper editors, bookstore
owners, florists and TV producers.

As they hurtled about the city by taxi Norma's
impression of Rome was rather kaleidoscopic.

The red bricks and golden stone of the Forum, the Colosseum, the Caracalla Baths, the Temple of Vesta, glowed in the mellow autumn sunshine. High on its hills the Capitoline Tower above the Senators' Palace, now the offices of the mayor, soared up commandingly. Behind it gleamed the huge white monument to King Victor Emmanuel II. Everywhere they went there was a baroque church with intricate carvings or a *piazza* with a fountain designed by a great sculptor. Everywhere too were the persistent little cars, streaming along streets, wide and narrow, or parked cheekily down the middles of boulevards or on pavements.

They lunched in a restaurant near the Spanish Steps, then took the Metro to E.U.R., a district on the outskirts of the old city that had been developed by Mussolini to house the Roman World Exhibition that was never held. It was a district of huge exhibition palaces, museums and sports complexes, stark modern buildings that owed much in their design to the architecture of ancient Rome and Greece, purely classical in their severity.

Pleased with the contacts they had made and assured that they had covered every detail of the arrangements for the book launching luncheon and that the rest could be done by phone or mail from London, they returned through the jostling noisy rush hour traffic to the hotel and went straight to one of the bars to have well-earned drinks and to check over together everything they had accomplished that day.

'So where shall we have dinner tonight?' Melinda asked when they had finished talking business.

'I have a dinner date already,' said Norma,

pushing a folder of papers into her briefcase.

'Oh, really? Where? With whom?' asked Melinda curiously. A woman in her early thirties, she was tall and slender and given to wearing flamboyant clothes. Today she was dressed in a long loose coat of bright purple ultra-suede that had a fur collar, and a purple wide-brimmed hat was tilted rakishly on her blonde hair. Her triangular face was daubed heavily with blusher and bluish-green eye-shadow was spread over her eyelids and also in the space above her eyes and below her pencilled-in eyebrows. 'With a man?' she added.

'Yes.'

'Where did you meet him?'

'Here, in Rome, yesterday afternoon,' replied Norma guardedly. She hoped Melinda wouldn't ask if she could join her and Roberto for dinner.

'I see.' Melinda took a long drink of her gin and tonic and gave her a long assessing glance. 'I hope you haven't been foolish enough to let yourself be picked up by an Italian gigolo,' she drawled. 'You're just the type one of them would go for—small, innocent-looking, red-haired, white-skinned. Quite a different dish from the swarthy, over-developed Italian girls.'

'Oh, no, nothing like that,' replied Norma with a merry little laugh. 'I'm not so easily taken in. He's—well, he's the son of an old friend of my mother,' she explained. 'I'm sorry I can't spend the evening with you. I hope you don't mind.'

'Not at all.' Melinda's smile was bright but somehow insincere. 'Dining alone goes with the territory when you're a business woman, doesn't it? I'm sure you've spent many an evening alone when you've had to go away on business from your home ground.' She laughed a little. 'I used to think I'd enjoy it, that I'd always find someone, preferably a man of course, to have dinner with. That's because I'd always assumed, I suppose, that that was how the men did it when they went away on business trips. I found out differently. The long evenings and nights away from home can be extremely lonely and boring.'

'Yes, I know what you mean,' said Norma, thinking of the few times she had spent in strange towns, wondering whether the business she had been sent to do had been really worth all the effort of uprooting herself from her flat and office in London. Then she remembered her mother who had had to spend so much time away from home in the course of her career as an opera singer. 'My mother used to be away a lot in her profession as an opera singer,' she said. 'I'm sure she must have always had company while she was away, but when she came home she used to say she was glad to be back because at home with me and my stepfather she could be herself. She could pretend she was nothing more than a wife and a mother and luxuriate in the freedom from outside pressures.'

'I suppose we have to have both—we women, I mean. We have to be able to go out to work so that we can enjoy being at home,' said Melinda, rising to her feet. 'I'll see you at breakfast, then. What time do you think we should leave to catch the train to Florence?'

'It leaves at nine and I'm told that Italian trains nearly always leave dead on time, so perhaps we should have breakfast at seven-thirty and book a taxi to pick us up at eight,' said Norma.

'Okay. Have a good time,' said Melinda, and drifted out of the bar.

Although she had plenty of time to shower and to get ready to go out Norma was late going down to the foyer to meet Roberto, mostly because she had been undecided about what she should wear and had frittered away time changing into and out of the various dresses and suits she had brought with her. In the end she chose a turqoise-coloured dress of pure silk crêpe-de-chine with a full skirt and a high neckline. Over it she wore a plain black woollen coat, and carrying suitable accessories she hurried to the elevator, leaving her room littered with the clothes she had discarded.

Roberto wasn't in the foyer when she reached it and for at least five minutes she stood alone watching the revolving doors swinging, wondering if he had changed his mind and had decided not to have dinner with her after all, or if he had forgotten he had made a date with her. Or perhaps he had arrived right on time at seven-thirty almost twenty minutes ago and not finding her waiting for him had left, annoyed because she had been late.

Surprised by the sinking sense of disappointment she felt because he wasn't there, she remained where she was, looking about disconsolately, feeling as if this was the first date with a man she had ever had and guessing that if he didn't come the rejection she would experience would be the worst she had ever felt in her life, and then wishing quite vehemently that she hadn't met him and so hadn't been placed in this forlorn situation.

'I hope you are waiting for me, *signorina*.'

The sound of the deep voice speaking behind her again sent frissons of excitement tingling along her nerves and her heart began to race. Blood rushed into her cheeks and she took a few seconds to turn to him because she didn't want him to see how pleased she was that he was there. Slowly she swung to face him.

He was formally dressed in an elegantly tailored slate-grey suit, white shirt and dark tie, and she was glad she had decided to dress up too. His long narrow eyes regarded her warily and his well-shaped lips with their somewhat sensual curve didn't smile.

'I . . . I thought that perhaps you'd forgotten you'd made a date to have dinner with me,' she whispered, aware of all sorts of vibrations quivering between them.

'And I thought you'd forgotten I had said I would come for you,' he replied, his voice very deep and soft now, his eyes looking right into hers, a tiny golden flame blazing in their depths. 'I've been here since twenty-five minutes after seven, and I've just phoned your room.'

'I must have left the room when you rang,' she explained, unable to look away from him, blood pounding in her ears and still flushing her cheeks, the pulse at the base of her throat leaping.

He also seemed to be mesmerised by her and they stood a few moments longer, looking at each other in silence, oblivious to the other people in the foyer, coming and going, talking and laughing. At last Roberto said,

'My car is parked right outside. We'd better go before someone starts complaining that it's in the way.'

A hand under her elbow, he guided her across the foyer to the revolving doors.

CHAPTER THREE

HIS car was the sports Ferrari, sleek and silvery, gleaming under the street lights and drawing the attention of many passers-by. Sitting in the front of it beside him, Norma was very much aware of his powerful physical presence, his arms brushing against hers, his hand touching her knee when he took hold of the gear lever between them.

Through narrow dark streets and around squares, thronged with crowds of Romans out for their usual evening walk either shopping or searching for restaurants, Roberto drove, like a Roman, quickly and without much regard for other drivers or for pedestrians, taking chances and determined to have his own way, until they reached a corner where two streets met by the river. There, also like other Romans, he abandoned the car rather than parked it, squeezed between two of the box-like Fiats, with its front wheels on the pavement.

His hand at her elbow again, he urged her along a street to a massive archway on either side of which flames flickered in antique torches. Huge oak doors dark with age and carved with some ancient coats of arms stood wide open, giving access into a small entrance hall. More modern, glass doors swung open at their approach. The doorman, wearing a maroon-coloured suit, bowed slightly.

'*Buona sera*, Signor Cortelli,' he greeted him.

The foyer was quiet, dimly lit. A footman, also in a maroon-coloured suit, came and took their coats and also greeted Roberto politely and by name. They went up to a wide staircase together.

'This is the residence of an old Roman family,' Roberto explained. 'It was built in the fourteenth century. As you can see, the panelling is very old. The tapestries hanging on the walls and some of the furniture used in the dining room are also antique. Descendants of the family live on the top floor and they own the restaurant. I hope you will enjoy it. The food is perhaps the best you will find in Rome.'

At the top of the stairs they were met by the head waiter, resplendent in black and white, who also made a positive identification of Roberto Cortelli and then led them through a large dining room where parties of people were sitting around tables talking and laughing. In a corner a pianist was playing a grand piano. Up three shallow steps the head waiter led them and into a small room, draped with colourful tapestries and lit by several antique wooden chandeliers in which real candles flickered. In this room tables were set only for two and they were shown to the table in the corner furthest away from the entrance.

Starched white linen gleamed, heavy silverware and glass goblets winked. Norma sat in the corner, the rich yet dark colours of the tapestry covering the wall behind her a perfect background for her glowing hair, white skin and turquoise dress. Roberto sat opposite to her, the boldly chiselled lines and planes of his lean dark face accentuated by the light that slanted across it.

Menus and the wine list were produced by two attentive waiters. Norma was consulted about her tastes in food and all of them made suggestions as to what she should choose to eat. They were all so kind and courteous that she felt as if she was the most important person in their lives at that moment and what she was going to eat a matter of great significance. When she had chosen Roberto ordered the wine. It was brought immediately, liquid gold in its tall bottle— Frascati, the wine of Rome, produced from grapes grown among the hills south of the city.

When the waiters had departed to the kitchen Roberto said:

'I had intended to take you to Alfredo's, near the ruins of Augustus's tomb.'

'You mean Alfredo who is famous for his *fettuccine*?' she asked.

'That is the one. I was going to show you the photographs on the walls there of Maria with my father and myself. I thought it would prove to you once and for all that I used to know her.'

'Why didn't you take me there?'

'I decided it would be too noisy and there would be too many people who know me. This is better. Here we will be undisturbed and can talk intimately.' He raised his wine glass. 'I drink to our better acquaintance tonight, Norma,' he added softly.

The sensually suggestive glance of his eyes was not lost on her, and her heart seemed to change rhythm. Never had any man looked at her as he was looking at her, as if he would have liked to have been more intimate with her.

'There is an opera called *Norma*. It is by Bellini,' he went on. 'Maria used to love to sing the part of Norma. Did you know that?'

'Yes. I have a recording of her singing in that opera.'

'And an aria from it was used in Louis Malle's film *Atlantic City*. Have you seen that film?' he asked.

'No, I haven't.' She sipped some wine.

'It was excellent, and won prizes at the Cannes Film Festival.' He paused also to sip wine and looked across at her again, his eyes sparkling with interest. His vitality seemed to leap across the table towards her and envelop her. She felt as if she was caught in a glittering net of magic that he had tossed around her from which she would never be free again. 'Do you sing, too? Like Maria?' he asked next.

'I croak like a bullfrog,' she admitted with a self-deprecatory smile, and felt a warm spurt of pleasure when he grinned back at her in appreciation of her remark. 'What about you? Did you follow in your father's footsteps?'

'No.' He shook his head. 'He would have liked me to. He insisted I sang in a boys' choir when I lived in New York with my mother. And he would give me singing lessons too when he was at home. But I didn't want to be an opera singer. I was too fascinated by the cinema. I used to spend all my pocket money going to the movies, and my ambition was to direct and make my own films one day, and when I came to live here in Rome with my father I took courses in film-making.'

'Have you made any films?' she asked.

Now it was his turn to grin self-mockingly.

'It would seem you have not seen them, or heard of me or my films. My fame has not yet reached London?'

'Oh, well, I don't go often to the films . . . and rarely to see foreign ones,' Norma began to excuse herself—then saw he was laughing at her.

'Please, do not apologise,' he said. 'I have made only two films so far that I can call my own. For a long time I was learning how to. When I left university here in Rome I went to Hollywood and began at the bottom doing any job I could as long as it was in a film studio so that I could watch some great film director at work. I even had small acting parts in a few films.'

'How long were you there?'

'About eight years. When I thought I knew enough I came back to Rome to work with Fellini. Now I make my own films at last. And since my father died and left me all his money I am independent, free to make the sort of films I want to make.'

'Were the two films you have directed successful?'

'Here in Italy they were, and possibly in France and Germany. But I am aiming for a more international audience, so the next film I make will be based on a story by a popular English woman writer. It is called *The Celebrity* and is about an English woman who comes to Rome to act in a film.'

'I've read it,' said Norma, now surging along on the waves of his infectious enthusiasm.

'Good, because you look something like I imagine the heroine of the story,' he said. 'Would you come to the film studios at Cinècitta tomorrow to take a screen test?'

'Me?' she exclaimed, then laughed, shaking her head. 'You can't be serious!'

'But I am. You would photograph well and you are unknown. It is best to use an unknown in the sort of film I want to make.'

'I couldn't possibly take a screen test tomorrow. I'm going to Florence tomorrow. Anyway, I don't think I'm like the woman in the story. I remember a description of her. It said she was very thin and had a pale face and mousy hair. My hair is certainly not mousy and I'm not undernourished!'

'I know that. But on film we can make you appear differently. It is your eyes that suggest to me that you would be perfect in the part.' He leaned forward. 'Come back to Rome when you have done what you have to do in Firenze and take the test,' he went on persuasively. 'Taking a screen test won't commit you to acting in the film. Nor will it commit me to giving you the part. But it will show whether you have any potential as a film actress.'

'No.' She shook her head again. 'After Florence we go to Venice and then to Milan, and then home.'

'We?' he queried.

'Melinda Morrison and I. She's the public relations director of a British publishing company and together we're making arrangements for the visit of another English writer to this country—Jeremy Jenson. Have you heard of him?'

'Yes, I have.' Interest sparked in his eyes. 'I have read his books. I like particularly the one about the invasion of Italy by the Allies during the last war. It would make a good film.' He sat back because the waiter had brought the first course of the meal and began to serve it.

From the other room the sound of the piano floated. The pianist was playing an arrangement of a romantic ballad, composed years ago but which Norma recognised. It was called *All the Things You Are*. The tune was a little sad, haunting.

She glanced across at Roberto Cortelli, but for once he wasn't looking at her. She thought of all the things he was or appeared to be. He was handsome, vigorous, ambitious and already an achiever. She doubted if he had ever let anyone stand in his way. She guessed also that he was chauvinistic in his attitude to women. Yet he also gave the impression that what you saw of him and what he let you know about him was not necessarily all of him. He held a lot of himself back. There was a depth to him, a secret part that he would share with no one. Not even with the woman he loved.

The woman he loved. There she went again, her thoughts turning surprisingly to romance. What would it be like to be the woman he loved, and why was she even considering the question? The wine, the romantic music, the intimacy of the situation here in this beautiful old room, just the two of them dining *tête-à-tête*, must be going to her head. She sat back quickly in her chair hoping that her thoughts which, for once, were very influenced by her emotions, weren't expressed in her eyes.

'You would be perfect in the part,' said Roberto suddenly, and she realised he had been watching her again. The waiters had departed. She picked up her fork and began to search in the *antipasto* she had ordered for tasty titbits of seafood.

'I can't act,' she said flatly.

'You don't have to be able to act. All you would have to do is learn the lines of the script and do as I tell you. You don't really believe that all the people you have seen in films can act, do you?' There was an edge of scorn to his voice. 'Some of them who are now film stars just happen to look well on the screen and do as they are told by the director of the film.'

'Like Christabel, the woman in the book.'

'That's right. It's what the book is about—the creation of illusion, and that is what making a film is all about.'

'But I don't want to be like the woman in the book,' she argued. 'I don't want to lose my identity and become unsure of who I am.' She drew an unsteady breath as she felt a return of the disappointment she had experienced in the foyer of the hotel when she had thought he had forgotten to come for her. 'Is that why you invited me out to dinner?' she asked. 'Just so you could persuade me to take a film test?'

He looked back at her, his eyes slits of darkness.

'No, that isn't why I invited you to have dinner,' he said softly, 'I invited you because I wanted to see you again and to talk with you. So what about you?' he went on challengingly. 'Did you accept my invitation because I said I would bring the letters to you?'

'Oh, no, that isn't why . . . I mean,' she was suddenly unaccountably flustered by his mocking glance, 'well, I do want the letters, but . . . but that isn't why I accepted your invitation,' she finished lamely. 'Have you brought them?'

'No.' He grinned ruefully. 'I forgot all about them and they are still locked in the desk drawer at my house.'

'Have you looked at them?'

'No, that too I forgot to do. I have been busy, looking for the right woman for my film. Do you really want them back?'

'Yes. You see, Roy asked me to take them back to him if I wasn't able to give them to the person who wrote them,' she explained.

'Then you will have to come back to the house with me after dinner if you really want them. Will you come home with me tonight, Norma?' he asked softly and suggestively.

Her pulses raced and her cheeks burned in response to this new invitation of his. If she went with him to the lovely old house on the other side of the river tonight she guessed he would try to seduce her. So shouldn't she refuse? Play safe?

She glanced at him stealthily from under her lashes and felt something deep within flare up, a flame of desire that flickered along her nerves, spreading through her. She ached suddenly to feel his hands upon her, his lips bruising hers. She yearned to touch him, to caress his face, slide her fingers through his hair, seek for and find the mystery of his lithe body hidden now from her beneath smooth wool and silk.

Shocked by the wantonness of her feelings, she laid down her fork and picked up her wine glass to empty it. Immediately Roberto filled the glass up again.

'You haven't answered my request, Norma,' he said. 'Will you come home with me after we've dined?'

'To ... to get the letters?' she queried, trying to assert some control over the desire that was leaping through her.

'But of course—to get the letters,' he replied smoothly, raising his glass to his lips over the rim of the glass, his eyes glinting at her mockingly. 'It is your only chance to get them before you go to Firenze.'

No longer did she hear the piano music, because there was a strange roaring in her ears. No longer did she see the white gleam of linen, the glitter of silverware and glass. She saw only dark eyes enticing her with their secret laughter and firm straight lips that had a wicked sensual curl to them.

'Yes, I'll come home with you,' she whispered.

It was midnight when they entered the house by a side door that opened on to another street. After locking and bolting the door Roberto took her hand and led her along a dimly lit narrow passage into the wide, high entrance hall. She knew it was midnight because a clock chimed the hour somewhere in the house; ancient silvery notes that added to the magic of the moment as they stepped into the centre of a spotlight shed by the moonlight that slanted in from a window high up in the domed roof.

Midnight. Time for Cinderella to go home. But she wasn't Cinderella and she had never wanted to be. She was a woman in control of her own destiny, free to make choices, and tonight she had chosen to come back to this house with Roberto.

Moonlight silvered his hair, the strong chiselled features of his face. It glinted in his eyes.

'You'll stay the rest of the night with me now that you're here,' he murmured, and it was an order rather than a request.

She made one last stand against the subtle attack he had made upon her ever since she had met him. Had it been only yesterday?

'I ... I don't think I can. I have to meet Melinda for breakfast at seven-thirty and leave for the station at eight. And I have to pack before I leave.'

'You'll meet her,' he said confidently, and framed her face with his hands.

It wasn't the first time Norma had felt the touch of those long fingers that evening, for after they had dined he had taken her dancing to a famous Roman night-club, where, surrounded by other dancers, they had swayed together cheek to cheek, forced into each other's arms by the crush, in intimate contact that had been merely the prelude to greater intimacy to come later.

'At sunrise I'll drive you back to the hotel,' he continued softly, sweeping away, even before she made them, any further arguments. 'I have much to do tomorrow too and must get up early. But the night is ours and we have six hours left to spend it together, learning about each other, loving each other. Do you agree to stay with me?'

His hands slid down her cheeks, drifted over her throat and down to her breasts.

'I agree,' she sighed, swaying towards him, lifting an arm about his neck and drawing his head down towards her, tilting her face up to his.

Their lips met in a kiss that was both gentle and demanding, hinting at the passionate feelings each of them was holding in check. As it deepened they both became impatient, both wanting more. Breathlessly, they stopped kissing as if by mutual agreement.

'Let's go to bed,' muttered Roberto thickly. 'I'll show you the way.' And taking her hand in his he pulled her after him towards the stairs.

Willingly Norma went with him to a room at the front of the house where moonlight glinted on mirrors, on the brass handles of old chests of drawers, and silvered the white sheets and pillows of the turned-down wide double bed. Right into the room he led her and kicked the door shut behind him, whirling her back into his arms, not waiting this time for her to show her willingness but claiming her lips in a kiss that bruised and dominated while his hands, roving over her, loosened the belt of her coat, slid it from her until it fell to the floor. Then his fingers found and slid open the zip at the back of her dress and that too joined her coat on the floor.

Slowly and gracefully, as if they were performing some sort of ritual dance, a dance of courtship, perhaps, they caressed each other, gradually smoothing away all articles of clothing until they were both bare and their skins were silvered by moonlight. And all the time their lips were feasting on each other's lips or in tender hollows where vulnerable nerves quivered at a touch. Pressed against the length of Roberto's lithe body, Norma felt every throb, every ripple of his mounting passion pass from him, through his warm velvety skin to her skin and through to her nerves, exciting wonderful sensations that set her head whirling and made her unsteady on her feet so that she had to cling to him.

Then he lifted her and carried her to the bed and, closely entwined with her, he continued to coax from her already tingling nerves exquisitely painful responses until she could no longer bear more of the pleasurable agony and sought with eager hands to invite him to do what he wanted to do, to plunge into her and move inside her until she was exploding with him in joyous ecstasy that left them both limp and laughing after its sudden violence, their excited hearts thudding in unison,

'You seem surprised,' whispered Roberto, rolling away from her on to his back, then reaching out a long arm to gather her against him until her head rested on his shoulder.

'I . . . I think I am,' she murmured. 'I didn't think it was possible to . . . to meet someone and . . . and . . .' She hesitated for a moment, searching for the right words to express how she felt, and could only find one way. 'I didn't think it was possible to fall in love so quickly,' she added shyly, placing her hand on his chest and curling her fingers to the froth of dark hairs. 'And to consummate that love the same day.'

'It has never happened to you before?' he asked casually, stroking her hair gently.

'No. I mean . . . I've been in love before, but . . . but not like this,' she muttered. 'I . . . I thought it happened only in books.'

'It happens to many people all the time,' he replied softly. 'Don't you know your Shakespeare? In *As You Like It* he expressed what happens in the best possible language. "*No sooner met but they looked, no sooner looked but they loved*," and later he says they sought the remedy for their sighs of longing.'

'You think that's what has happened to us?' she asked, wanting him to say he loved her.

'I know it has. My only regret is that we have so little time, that we have only tonight. Must you go to Firenze tomorrow?'

'Yes. If I don't go Melinda will complain to my employer and I might lose my job.'

'And you wouldn't like that? You wouldn't count the world well lost for love, like Mark Antony and Cleopatra?' he asked rather mockingly, shifting over on to his side so that they lay facing each other, their bodies shadowed and silvered, mysteriously tempting.

'No, I wouldn't. I like my work and I don't want to lose the job I have. I might get promoted if I do this work in Italy very well.'

'Then we must make the most of tonight,' he whispered, tipping his head towards hers until their foreheads touched and his lips were only a few inches from hers. His hand stroked her bare shoulder, then slid slowly down her arm, greedily caressing the silkiness of her skin. 'Let's make love while we can, sweet Norma. "*In delay there lies no plenty*," to quote your Shakespeare again.'

'You seem to know his plays very well.'

'I majored in English literature when I was at university here in Rome,' and his lips took hers again, effectively smothering a suspicion that briefly leapt up in her mind.

Under more caresses of his hands and lips desire unfolded and blossomed slowly and beautifully, as the bud of a flower unfurls its petals to the warmth of the sun, and burst from her in a shower of shattering sensations, and afterwards, amazed by her complete surrender to his lovemaking, she slept peacefully, curled up against him.

Next morning, true to his word, Roberto woke her early and drove her at sunrise across the river towards the sun-gilt city. They sat in silence. Norma was silent because she was afraid that if she spoke she would break down and say she wanted to stay with him and not go to Florence. He was silent, she guessed, because his thoughts had already moved on and away from her and were busy with what he had to do that day. The night of loving was over. Sunrise had brought a return to reality and the parting of their ways.

When he stopped the car outside the hotel she turned to him, knowing he was impatient to drive on yet wishing to delay him just a little longer to ask him if she would ever see him again.

'Will I . . .' she began, and had to stop because her throat closed up. All she could do was look at him, hoping her expression was saying all she couldn't put into words.

He turned to her. His eyes softened and darkened. His fingers touched her cheek, their tips cool against her skin.

'*Arrivederci*, Norma. Until we meet again,' he whispered, and against her lips his were cool and swift. 'Enjoy Firenze,' he added, lifting his head and moving back into his seat.

Pride came to her aid then, helping her through the difficult moment while her instincts were shrieking to her to reach out and hold him and never let him go.

'I will,' she said, smiling cheerfully. She opened the door and swung her legs out of the car. 'Goodbye.'

She stood up. The door of the car slammed shut, then the vehicle shot away from the kerb into the traffic that was already streaming along the Via Veneto, and she turned quickly to enter the hotel, trying to pretend that her eyes weren't brimming with tears.

CHAPTER FOUR

THE train sped smoothly along gleaming rails through the green countryside. Rows of vines marched in straight lines across the lower slopes of hills. In the distance the shape of an old castle was silhouetted on the top of a hill against the hazy grey sky. The train entered a tunnel and Norma closed her eyes, her heart seeming to throb in time to the clatter of wheels.

Not enough sleep. Not enough sleep. Not enough sleep. The words pounded through her head in time to the rhythm of the wheels too. And why hadn't she had enough sleep? Because she had spent most of the night making love with a man she had known for only a day and a half.

She still couldn't believe it had happened. She still couldn't believe she had deliberately chosen to go back to Roberto's house with him, guessing that he would make love to her and she would sleep with him. She still couldn't believe that she, Norma Seton, who was considering marriage to Aubrey Brenton, whom she had known for over three years, who had always prided herself on her independence of spirit, and who had always refused to be intimate with a man unless he offered marriage, had fallen in love so completely and desperately with Roberto Cortelli whom she hadn't known or met until the day before yesterday. And more than that, more than falling in love with him, she had broken her own rule of personal morality and had allowed him to pleasure himself with her body.

Would she ever see him again? The chances were very slim. He lived in Rome and she lived in London. He was engrossed in his career as a film director and she was involved with her career in public relations. To meet again, to be together, they would have to make deliberate arrangements. They would have to take time off from their work so they could escape to paradise for a few days. Or hours. Unless one of them was willing to give up a career to go and live where the other lived.

The train hurtled out of the tunnel and she opened her eyes again. Melinda was sitting opposite her, the magazine she had been reading laid down on her knees, her blue-green eyes narrowed between thickly mascaraed lashes under the brim of yet another rakish hat, black this time with a narrow band of white matching the black white-trimmed suit she was wearing.

'Did you have a good time last night?' asked Melinda, putting aside the magazine. They were the only occupants of the compartment and so could talk freely and frankly.

'Yes, thank you,' said Norma politely. 'Did you?'

'So-so.' Melinda shrugged her shoulders, opened her handbag and took out a cigarette case and lighter. 'Mind if I smoke? It isn't a non-smoking compartment.'

'No, go ahead. Where did you go for dinner? Did you stay at the hotel?'

'I went to Alfredo's. It was a lot of fun.' Her cigarette lit, Melinda blew out smoke. Behind the grey veil of it her eyes were sharp and curious. 'I saw him, you know,' she continued. 'I saw you meet him in the foyer. He's quite gorgeous, and I'm not at all surprised you spent the night with him. I would have, too, given half the chance.'

Jolted by the remark, Norma stiffened in her seat and opened her eyes wide.

'How . . . how . . .' she spluttered.

'How do I know you spent the night with him?' said Melinda with a smug smile. 'I didn't know— I only guessed at what would happen when I saw the way you and he looked at each other. *Whew!*' She pursed her lips in a whistle. 'It was something else—talk about torrid! And yet in a way you don't strike me as being the sort of woman who goes in for one-night stands.'

Norma looked away from the other woman's probing gaze and stared out at the countryside through which the train was passing, hardly seeing it.

A one-night stand—the words seemed to stab her right through to the heart. Was that what the hours spent with Roberto had been? A one-night affair? Had she fallen a victim to the charm of a Latin lover after all? Had she been wined and dined and seduced in a few hours and then been forgotten?

Oh God, no, surely not! Surely there had been more to it than that. Surely it hadn't been just a case of lust in action, a satisfying merely of physical appetites. No, no, it couldn't have been only a short-term aberration of the senses.

She looked back at Melinda. The blue-green eyes looked at her. Outwardly Melinda appeared to be the epitome of the sophisticated liberated woman, experienced, hardened and cynical, hardly someone in whom she could confide or whom she would want to ask for advice about love.

'I'm not the sort of woman who goes in for one-night stands,' she said with a touch of dignity. 'It wasn't what you think.'

'Oh?' Melinda's glance was sceptical. 'Are you going to see him again, then?'

Norma suddenly remembered the letters. They were still locked up in the desk at Roberto's house. He had forgotten to give them to her and she had forgotten to ask him for them. He and she had been so wrapped up in each other, so consumed by the flare-up of attraction between them, that they had forgotten everything else. She would have to phone him from Florence and ask him to send the letters to her address in London. The letters gave her a legitimate excuse to get in touch with him again. Her spirits lifted. Everything seemed so much brighter and she felt less tired. Even Melinda didn't seem quite so cynical and sceptical.

'Yes, I am going to see him again,' she said positively. 'He has something belonging to my mother that he had to return to me.'

'Oh, I see. Will you see him again before we leave Italy?' asked Melinda.

'I don't know. I'm not sure,' said Norma coolly. 'I can hear the train attendant announcing the first sitting for lunch. We have tickets for that, so shall we go along to the restaurant?' she added, rising to her feet, glad of the opportunity to change the subject of conversation.

They shared a table with an American couple who were on holiday and touring Europe, and the hour passed quickly as the four of them chatted, sharing experiences of travel in different countries. When Melinda and she returned to their own compartment Norma made every effort to keep the conversation impersonal, discussing their plans for the Florence book-launching luncheon.

'I'd like, if possible, to keep some time free tomorrow morning,' said Melinda. 'I'd like to go to the Uffizi Gallery, and you know all the public galleries and museums are closed in the afternoon. Are you interested?'

'Yes, I am. It doesn't seem right to visit Florence and not see some of the world's most famous paintings,' said Norma. 'Well, if we can finish making arrangements at the hotel we'll be staying at to hire the ballroom there for the February luncheon this afternoon, we could leave the media people, the florist and the bookstores to do either early in the morning or later tomorrow afternoon. That would give us some time for the Uffizi. Do you still want to go to Venice on Thursday?'

'It would be a pity to have come all this way and not go there on our days off,' said Melinda. 'All expenses paid, too.'

'I suppose so,' agreed Norma.

Once they arrived in Florence everything seemed to happen very quickly. From the station they were whisked by taxi to their hotel, which was situated not far from the station on a small *piazza* close to the main shopping areas. They spent the rest of the afternoon in a meeting with the catering manager of the hotel and inspecting the ballroom and discussing what food would be served at the luncheon. The bookings of rooms were made, and after changing their clothes they set out together to walk the streets with crowds of Florentines and tourists.

Finding their way to the Piazza del Duomo, the heart of the city, they stared with awe at the huge Cathedral with its magnificent dome, designed and erected by the architect Brunelleschi in the fifteenth century and which ever since has been acclaimed as one of the great architectural wonders of the world. At one side of the green, white and red marble building was the graceful bell-tower designed by Giotto in the fourteenth century, also faced in coloured marbles. Then, in the gathering dusk, they crossed the road to one of the oldest surviving buildings of the city, the Baptistry. Octagonal in shape, it also had a typically Tuscan Romanesque green and white facing and was famous for its three doors on the north, south and east sides, the east door being the most famous. Created by the sculptor Lorenzo Ghiberti and showing scenes from the Bible and cast in bronze, it had been nicknamed 'the Gate of Paradise' by the famous sculptor and architect Michelangelo, who had also been born in Florence.

Along narrow streets lined by tall fourteenth-century buildings they walked, passing massive iron-studded doors and secretive windows covered by heavy iron grilles, until they reached the river Arno where the Ponte Vecchio was reflected perfectly in the smooth lamplit water. Leaving the bridge, they walked back down another narrow street and found themselves in a wide open square, the Piazza della Signoria, where, it seemed, all the youth of Florence had gathered for the evening to talk or play soccer. In a corner of the *piazza* they lingered under the formidable walls of the Palazzo Vecchio, the city hall, originally started in the early fourteenth century and added to in subsequent centuries. Tilting back their heads, they viewed the impressive and austere clock tower silhouetted against the sunset-flushed evening sky.

They dined at a small restaurant where the service was brisk yet friendly and the food was excellent, then returned to the hotel along narrow streets. Pleading tiredness, Norma went straight to her room. Within a few minutes she was on the phone and waiting for a long-distance call to be put through to the house on the Via Scipione in Rome.

When at last she heard a voice she suspected was Paolo's she asked him if she could speak to Roberto.

'Signor Cortelli is not at home,' answered the old servant.

'May I leave a message for him?'

'*Si.*'

'This is Signorina Norma Seton calling,' she spoke slowly and carefully. 'Would you please ask Signor Cortelli to phone me at the Baglioni Hotel in Florence tomorrow, in the evening? This is the phone number of the hotel and my room number. Do you understand?'

'*Si, signorina.* I write everything down. I will tell him. *Buona sera.*'

Paolo rang off before she could say anything else. She put down the receiver. She hoped he had written down the message correctly.

The next day was cool but sunny. After calling on the local TV station and discussing with the producer of the local news programme the forthcoming luncheon and visit of Jeremy Jenson and the launching of the Italian translations of his books, Norma and Melinda went to the Uffizi Gallery and stayed there until it closed, viewing such famous original paintings as *The Birth of Venus* and the *Primavera* by Botticelli, as well as several masterpieces by Titian and Tintoretto and Raphael. They left the gallery reluctantly, wishing they had had more time to consider the beauties of the paintings they had seen and absolutely overawed by the numerous exquisite works of art the gallery contained.

They lunched standing up in a small *trattoria* with other busy people, wolfing down sandwiches of crusty bread and slices of Parma ham which they washed down with cups of hot and creamy *capuccino*. Then they visited the rest of the people they had to see. Once again they spent the time after five o'clock until it was time to have dinner at eight in true Italian style, walking around the streets and window-shopping as well as buying. Melinda treated herself to a pair of leather boots from the Gucci shop and Norma bought herself a shawl. They also visited the outlet of a famous leather factory where they both bought handbags.

After dinner they walked to the Piazza della Signoria again to watch the evening activities there and to admire the sculptures in the Loggia dei Lanzi, a place of graceful arches, where the statue of Perseus with the head of the Medusa by Benvenuto Cellini held pride of place. Back at the hotel they went to their separate rooms after agreeing to meet early next morning for breakfast before catching the train to Venice.

There had been no message for Norma at the reception desk in the foyer when she had asked for the key to her room. It seemed that no one had phoned her while she had been out. But there was still plenty of time for Roberto to phone, she argued with herself as she packed her case so that she would be ready for a quick getaway in the morning.

Maybe Paolo hadn't understood her message after all, she thought disconsolately as she got into bed. Or maybe Roberto had received the message but had decided to ignore it. She checked the time. It was almost midnight. Was it too late for her to phone him? Not really. Her hand was on the receiver when she remembered it had been midnight when he and she had returned to his house only two nights ago. Perhaps she should wait for a while. But then if she phoned him after midnight might she not disturb his sleep? *Might she not disturb him making love to another woman?*

The thought seemed to screech through her mind, shattering her. Oh, God, what had she done? Why had she stayed the night with him and slept with him? Why had she given in to passion? She must forget him, forget the hours they had spent together. Or remember their brief romance as a mistake to be learned from, but not to be regretted or to be ashamed of.

She had switched off the light and was trying to go to sleep when she thought she heard someone knocking on her door. She flicked on the bedside lamp again and listened. The knocking came again, more loudly. Scrambling off the bed, deciding that it must be Melinda who was knocking because no one else except the desk clerk knew the number of her room, she went to the door and opened it slightly, flinging it wide and gasping with a mixture of delight and surprise when she saw Roberto standing outside. He was wearing his grey suede jacket and jeans. His face was pale, his eyes red-rimmed, his hair tousled. He walked straight past her into the room without waiting to be invited and ordered her to shut the door quickly.

'How did you get here?' she asked weakly, following him.

'I drove.' Unzipping his jacket to reveal that he was wearing a highnecked grey sweater, he turned to face her. 'I didn't get your message asking me to come to you until late this morning. I left Rome immediately.' Taking off the jacket, he tossed it down on a chair and stepped closer to her, placing his hands on her shoulders and gazing down into her eyes.

'But I didn't ask you to come,' she said. 'I only asked you to phone me.'

He frowned in puzzlement, lines of weariness etched plainly in his face, at the corners of his eyes and down his cheeks.

'Paolo wrote the message down,' he said. 'It was written quite clearly. I was to come to you in Florence. So I came, and here I am.'

'Oh, I had a feeling he hadn't understood what I said to him,' she sighed.

'He understood enough to get the hotel and your room number down correctly,' said Roberto with a slight grin.

'I phoned you last night,' Norma explained, 'to ask you to send the letters to me in London, but you weren't in, so I asked Paolo to give you a message to phone me this evening. I've been waiting for you to phone, and now you're here. Oh, what can I say to you? I'm sorry, really sorry you drove all that way for nothing. . . .'

'I didn't come all that way for *nothing*. I came for this,' he said softly, his hands sliding along her shoulders to her throat and upwards to cup her face.

She had a glimpse of his eyes heavy-lidded and storm-grey, and then his lips were against hers. She responded helplessly, her arms going around his neck. His hands slid over her back, their heat passing through the thinness of her nightgown to her skin as he pressed her against him. At that intimate contact passion flared within her. With a little moan of pleasure she rubbed herself against him, her breasts tingling against his chest, her hips grinding against his, her mind taken over by the sensual delight of being close to him. The scents of his hair and skin filled her nostrils, the tough wiriness of his hair wound around her fingers and his lips bruised hers with a violent hunger.

Reluctantly his lips left hers and he raised his head.

'So aren't you glad Paolo made a mistake?' he asked. 'Aren't you glad I came to you instead of phoning you?'

'Yes, I am. But I hope you've brought the letters too. Have you?'

'No.' He shook his head and the smile in his secretive eyes mocked her.

'Oh, really—how could you forget them?' she demanded, stepping back from him.

'Easily. My mind was full of you and what we would do together once I was with you again,' he said. 'I forgot the letters, but I remembered that you had told me you had a free day before going to Milan, so I came to spend that day with you.' He rubbed his eyes with long fingers, sighed deeply and then dragged his fingers through his hair. 'But first I must sleep,' he said. He glanced sideways at the two beds that were pushed close together to become one bed if necessary. 'The beds look comfortable,' he remarked, going around to the side of the bed that she hadn't slept on.

'But you can't sleep here!' she exclaimed.

'Why not?' He began to take off his sweater.

'The hotel people—they won't like it. The room is reserved only for one person and . . .'

'They won't know.' His shirt was off now and following his sweater to the floor. In the lamplight his olive skin had a tint of bronze. Muscles rippled beneath skin as he moved. Norma stared in fascination, longing to reach forward and stroke his back, her fingertips remembering the velvety feel of it.

'No one saw me come in and no one will see me leave this room,' he drawled. His trousers dropped to the floor and, clad only in underbriefs, he pulled back the bedclothes and slid into the bed. 'Don't worry about it, *cara mia*,' he added drowsily as he settled his head on the pillow. 'Trust me. No one will know I slept in this room tonight.'

He fell asleep while she was trying to think up

some argument, and after a while, realising there was nothing she could do about it, laughing to herself about his cool assumption that he was welcome to share this room with her for the night, Norma got into the other bed and switched off the light again. In a few seconds she was also asleep, serene in the knowledge that she had only to stretch out a hand to touch him.

She was wakened six hours later by the shrill sound of the phone bell. Raising heavy eyelids, she stared at the white instrument on the bedside table, wondering vaguely why it was ringing so early when the sun was only just rising. Then she remembered she had asked to be called early so that she could meet Melinda for breakfast before catching the train to Venice.

The bell shrilled again and she lifted the receiver and muttered into it sleepily. The desk clerk on duty gave her a cheerful '*Buon giorno*,' and told her it was six-thirty. She thanked him, replaced the receiver and closing her eyes tried to doze off again.

'Who was that?' asked a deep lazy voice quite near to her.

Her eyelids flew up. She turned her head and saw rumpled black hair, a lean dark face that needed shaving and narrow dark grey eyes watching her through down-drooping black lashes. So she hadn't dreamed he had come. He was there beside her. He was really there.

'The desk clerk. I asked for an early call— Melinda and I are catching the train to Venice this morning.'

'Melinda is, but you're not,' Roberto said arrogantly, leaning up on an elbow and shifting so that he was close to her. 'You're spending the day with me. We have places to go and see.'

'But I have a train ticket and a seat reservation and a room booked in a Venetian hotel for tonight,' she argued. 'I can't not go. What will Melinda think if I don't go with her?'

'I don't know and I don't care,' he said, leaning over her and stroking back the hair from her brow which he kissed gently and almost reverently while his fingers slipped inside the opening in her nightgown and most irreverently began to caress her breast.

He looked down into her eyes, his own dark and sultry. Norma looked back. A breathless hush trembled between them.

'Let us make the most of today,' he whispered. 'Starting now.'

'Oh, yes, let's make the most of today,' she agreed wholeheartedly, sliding her hands over the smoothness of his hard shoulders and giving herself up to the smothering heat of his kiss and the skin-tingling caresses of his hands.

Passion flared up beyond all their expectations and satisfaction was a joyous mind-reeling fusion of excited emotions and physical sensations. Purged of longing, they lay afterwards in lazy contentment, their legs entwined, their hands still caressing heated skin, their lips occasionally nibbling in enticing hollows and against smooth curves.

Through a haze Norma heard again the shrill of the phone. Without turning away from Roberto she stretched out her free hand and felt for the receiver.

'Hello,' she said.

'Norma?' Melinda's voice rasped like a file against steel. 'What the hell are you doing? It's nearly eight-thirty and the taxi is here to take us to the station. The train will be leaving soon for Venice. Hurry up!'

Roberto moved, sliding away from her and sitting up. She covered the mouthpiece with her hand.

'It's Melinda,' she whispered. 'What shall I say to her?'

'Tell her you're not going with her to Venice, that you have better things to do and that you'll see her in Milan tomorrow,' he replied auto-cratically, laying down the law confidently as he got off the bed and wrapped a sheet round his body, toga-style. He went away in the direction of the bathroom. Much to her own surprise Norma obeyed his instructions, speaking rather breathlessly to Melinda.

'I've decided not to go to Venice.'

'*What*?' Melinda's shout was incredulous. 'Not go? But the trip is all paid for!'

'I know—I'm sorry. I'll claim on insurance for the cancellation of the bookings for me. I'll see you in Milan tomorrow afternoon.'

'I'll believe that when I see you in the Hilton Hotel foyer bar at six tomorrow evening—and not a minute later, or I'll be writing a complaint to Bright & Stevens about your behaviour on this trip!'

The receiver crashed down at the other end of the line and Norma winced. She returned her receiver to its rest and slid off the bed. Picking up her nightgown from the floor, she slipped it on and went over to the clothes closet where her dressing gown still hung. As she passed the open bathroom door an arm reached out and she was grabbed and jerked into the steam-filled room that was noisy with the sound of running water.

Naked, his skin beaded with moisture, his hair sleek and wet, Roberto laughed down at her, teeth flashing white in his unshaven dark face, his eyes glinting with devilry.

'It's time we took a shower together,' he said, and scooping her up in his arms he stepped into the bathtub.

CHAPTER FIVE

It was a day Norma would always remember as long as she lived, a golden capsule of time, separate from the past and from the future, in which she was caught and held spellbound for a few hours from the moment they drove away from Florence across the river, through narrow twisting streets in which there was hardly room for two cars to pass each other, until they were in the superbly landscaped Tuscan countryside.

Tall cypress trees, spear-shaped, marched along the crests of gently rolling hills. Oak trees glowed orange in contrast with the shimmering silvery green of olives. Vineyards were everywhere, dark lines crossing golden-brown earth. The same raw sienna colour was repeated in the stone walls of old villas and churches. On distant hilltops the tiled roofs of walled villages shimmered.

'It's like being in a painting by Raphael,' remarked Norma.

'So you have had time to visit the art galleries?' queried Roberto, glancing sideways at her.

'Only the Uffizi. And we didn't have time to do it justice. There's so much to see, I felt dizzy when I came out.' She half turned in her seat to look at him properly, studying the high forehead, the swept-back black hair, the prominent cheekbones, the straight nose, the elegant line of his jaw, the firmly moulded lips. 'I saw you in the gallery,' she said softly.

'Me?' He was startled out of his usual composure, as she had intended he should be, and she smiled impishly. He gave her another sidelong glance, noticed her smile and began to smile himself. 'I think perhaps you have a joke,' he remarked. 'Are you going to share it with me?'

'I saw you, and yet the man I saw wasn't you. In one of the rooms in the gallery there are a lot of paintings by Titian. Have you been there?' she asked.

'No. For me this is the first time in Tuscany. The first time too in Firenze, although I have often wanted to come. So go on about the paintings by Titian.'

'There were several portraits of people who were well known at the time he was painting—I forget their names. But among them was a painting of a man without a name. You could have posed for it. I kept going back to look at it. He was dressed in black velvet and his hair was like yours and he was looking over his shoulder at the artist, so he was looking over his shoulder at me. He was looking at me just as you look at me sometimes, as if . . .' She paused, not knowing how to describe how he looked at her.

'As if what?' he asked.

'Oh, it's hard to describe. You look at me as if . . . well, as if you know things about me that I don't know about myself and as if knowing them without me knowing gives you some sort of secret pleasure.'

Again Roberto gave her a glance over his shoulder, his eyes narrow, almost wary.

'I do know things about you,' he said, and his voice had a velvety tone, warm and sensuous. 'I know many lovely things that perhaps you don't know about yourself, many things that give me secret pleasure, *cara mia*.' He glanced quickly at the road ahead, then took hold of her nearest hand and lifting it to his lips, brushed the back of it with his lips. Her cheeks flamed in reaction to his lover's speech, to the burning glance he gave her, to the touch of his lips against her skin.

'You mustn't say that to me,' she whispered.

'Why not?' He was concentrating on driving again.

'I ... I'm not your ... your darling, your love.'

'But you are ... at least while we are together, you are. You were this morning at the hotel.' He gave her another glinting glance, full of devilry, and again her cheeks grew hot at this reference to the abandon of their lovemaking that morning. She looked out of the window beside her, trying to subdue the feelings of delight that his looks and his words aroused in her, warning herself that he was a master at the art of making love. It was an art that had been bred in his blood, in his bones.

'But I'm interested in the portrait of a man you think looked like me. You are quite sure he had no name?' he asked, cool and reserved again.

'Quite sure. His portrait was among the portraits of women, of some Duchess with her two daughters.'

'He was the Duke, perhaps?'

'Oh, no. The Duke was on the other side of the room with some of his male friends and a portrait of his mistress.' She gave him another teasing glance. 'Melinda suggested that maybe the unknown man was the Duchess's boy-friend.'

'So, maybe she was right,' he said, with another sidelong glance and a grin. 'And maybe he was an ancestor of mine. Who knows? You see, my father was born in Tuscany and the family of Cortelli lived for many hundreds of years in the district around San Gimignano. That is where we are going now. I have often wanted to see the town where he was born and to find the house where my grandparents used to live before they moved to Rome. You have heard of San Gimignano?'

'No. Is it famous for something?'

'For its towers and for its wine.'

'Towers?' she queried.

'*Sì*. Soon you will see them rising up from the top of a hill. There used to be seventy-two of them, but now there are only fourteen, so I am told. They were built by various rich and powerful families of the town. The greater the prestige of the family the higher the tower. It was the same in Firenze too, at one time.'

'Does the house where your father was born have a tower?' asked Norma.

'Not any more. It was destroyed, my father told me. Look—straight ahead. There is the town.'

There was a green hill at the top of which were walls. Over the tops of the walls several straight towers, straight and square, soared upwards, gleaming gold in the sunlight, looking for all the world like miniature skyscrapers.

As they drove closer to it the hill seemed to

shrink down. The towers lost their height and disappeared among olive orchards that covered the lower slopes of the hill. The road wound upwards and ended suddenly in an elliptical *piazza* planted with lawns and trees and shrubs outside the high golden-brown walls of the town.

Leaving the car parked in the square, they entered the town by way of a gateway in the walls and walked up a paved street edged with high narrow buildings, many of which had shops on their ground floors, until they reached a small square with a cistern or well in the middle. From this square a narrow passage led them into the main square where three tall towers built of grey stone glittered in the sunlight.

'As you can see, the two towers on the left are the same height and the same width,' said Roberto, after consulting his guide-book. 'They are known as the Salvucci twins. It seems that a statute was passed, long ago, prohibiting the construction of any towers higher than the first tower that was built, the Rognosa, which was fifteen metres high. But the Salvucci family disobeyed the statute by building two towers, and the sum of their height was superior to that of the Rognosa.'

'How very clever and crafty of them!' commented Norma. 'Which is the Rognosa tower?'

'That one. It is next to the Town Hall or Palace of the Podesta.'

'And where is the house where your father was born?'

'We go this way, down the Via San Matteo.'

The street was flanked by golden-brown buildings that had once belonged to wealthy families, judging by their graceful mullioned windows and arched doorways. Halfway along it they came to another narrower street and turned into that. The houses were high and narrow, their roofs almost touching high above the roadway, creating a tunnel almost. Roberto stopped outside the narrowest house. Its door was closed and blinds were drawn down behind its narrow windows.

'This is it?' asked Norma.

'This is it. My father didn't live here for long. When he was five his father and mother moved first to Siena and then to Rome. Grandfather was a musician too, an organist and choirmaster—and very ambitious for his only son, my father, when he discovered that son had a great voice.'

'He sounds like my mother's mother. She was Italian too, you know,' said Norma. 'And when she found my mother could sing in tune she sent her for singing lessons, to learn opera, and later she encouraged my mother, after my father was killed, to go to Rome to learn from your father. Are you going to knock on the door and tell the people in the house that your father was born here?'

He knocked, but there was no reply, and after a while someone came out of the house across the street to tell them that the family who lived in the Cortelli house were away for the day to Florence.

'What a pity,' said Norma as she and Roberto walked back to the town square.

'It doesn't matter,' Roberto shrugged. 'I can come back another time. One day I hope to make a film about my father, so I will be back.'

'Oh, what a coincidence!' exclaimed Norma.

'Roy, my stepfather, is going to write a biography of my mother. You and he should meet. You each have information that the other could use.'

'I suppose we do,' he replied noncommittally. 'Shall we have lunch now and then go up to the ruins of the old fort to look at the views?'

They lunched in a small restaurant in the square where they ate *cannelloni* and shared a bottle of San Gimignano wine. Afterwards they crossed the square again in the mellow autumn sunshine and turning right past the Cathedral, they found the market place silent and empty at that time of rest, with a few cars parked in it under the shade of two pine trees.

From the square they went up a flight of shallow steps to the gardens planted about the ruins of the old fort of Montestaffoli and from there mounted a narrow flight of steps cut into the side of a wall, to the top of one of the ruined round towers of the fortress.

From one side of the tower they could see the fourteen sunburnt towers of the town, rising straight as lances above the tiled roofs of the houses. Silent and inscrutable, each tower seemed like a sentinel protecting the town. From the other side of the fortress the hillside fell away steeply, covered in olive trees, to the beautiful sweep of a wide valley, a patchwork of brown fields, greyish-green olive orchards, dark vineyards and woods that flaunted autumn colours, rust, bronze, and orange.

'It's so quiet here,' said Norma. 'So peaceful. It's as if time had stopped in the fourteenth century. Up here on this hill enclosed by walls I feel safe and protected.'

'Do you want to feel safe?' Roberto asked. 'I thought you liked the rough-and-tumble of business life, of pitting your wits and know-how against other people in the same line as yourself.'

'I do. But there are times when I like to escape and to be quiet with someone I like and can feel at home with. Did your father ever come back here to see his birthplace?'

'Not as far as I know. He was so busy travelling from one country to another in the course of his career as a singer that when he retired he didn't leave Rome. He loved that city and the old house he had inherited, and I think he really retired from opera because he wanted to stay in one place.'

'Did your mother travel with him when he was singing?'

'She did when they were first married, but after their first child was born she stayed put too, on Long Island where she had been born. She's still there.'

'Oh. Didn't she ever live in Rome?'

'No. When my father retired she wanted him to stay on Long Island with her, but he refused and she wouldn't come to live in Rome, so they split. I came with him.'

'How old were you then?'

'Thirteen. My elder sister Gianetta stayed with my mother.'

'I suppose you go to visit your mother, though.'

'Not often. She doesn't like me since I preferred to live with my father than to live with her.' Roberto spoke coolly and curtly and shrugged as he turned away from her to look at the towers again. 'The sun is beginning to go down,' he said. 'Look how different the light is now on the towers. It's nearly time for us to leave.'

Norma moved closer to him. Their time together was almost over, but she didn't want it to end. She wanted the golden moments to last for ever. She wanted to stay with him in that place of ancient towers and protective walls and to be a part of its peaceful unhurried way of life.

'Thank you for coming and for bringing me here. I'll never forget this town,' she whispered, and meant that she would never forget him. Her hand sought his for comfort. Around her fingers his gripped strongly and for a few more moments they were as close in spirit as they ever could be. Roberto turned to face her, and high above the rooftops and the rich valley they looked at each other with longing while among the tall towers the evening breeze sang a sad song.

'It has been my pleasure to come to you and to bring you here. I won't forget either,' he said softly, lifting his other hand, touching her cheek, her lips, with his fingertips. Then with a gruff urgency that surprised her he said, 'Come back with me to Rome, tonight. Come and live with me there.'

His demand rocked her where she stood. She was aware of a fierce joy leaping up in her because he had asked her to live with him. It was followed by a burning desire to give in to his demand and grant his request, to cast off independence and freedom of action and surrender unconditionally to him, go where he wanted to go, live where he wanted to live.

'You ... you're going back to Rome tonight?' she exclaimed, stalling for time while she got her emotions under control.

'I have to go. There are people I must see tomorrow, film people. Come back with me and take that screen test.'

The flames of joy and passion sank down. It wasn't for herself he wanted her to go with him after all. It was for what he hoped he could get from her, an agreement to take the film test and perhaps appear in his next film.

'No, I can't,' she said firmly, unlinking her fingers from his and stepping apart from him, gazing at the towers again. The lower parts of the stone edifices were in the shadow now but the upper parts gleamed with coppery light as the rays of the setting sun struck them. 'I have to go to Milan. I have people to see, too, and work to do.'

'But you don't want to go,' he argued. 'You'd like to be with me. You want me as much as I want you, so why not come to Rome with me?'

'I can't—I can't!' she cried. 'I have to go to Milan or I'll lose my job.'

'This job of yours is more important then than I am ... more important than us? More important than what we have going between us?'

His voice was deep and purring, his eyes dark and sultry as he took hold of her shoulders and drew her towards him. His lips took hers in a sense-inflaming kiss that lasted too long for her peace of mind, a kiss that went on and on, seeming to penetrate right to the core of her being until she lost all knowledge of place and time.

Then it was over and she was staring up at him, her hand across her throbbing lips as she struggled to catch her breath. Roberto looked back at her as if he knew much about her that she didn't know. He looked at her as if he owned her.

'So what is your answer now, Norma?' he said suggestively. 'Is your work still more important to you than what is going on between us?'

'Yes, yes, it is ... it has to be. Isn't your work more important to you than I am, than what has happened between us? Would you give it up to come with me to Milan or back to England?' she challenged him.

Tiny golden flames seemed to blaze momentarily in the darkness of his storm-grey eyes and then were gone. He looked beyond her at the towers and his mouth quirked at one corner.

'No, I would not,' he replied coolly. His glance came back to her face, appraised it critically. 'You are not so unlike Maria as I had thought,' he remarked. 'She was also afraid of love.' He shrugged again and turned away from her. 'Let's go back to the car.'

In a cool silence created by the clash between them they walked back through the square where people were now gathering to sit on benches and talk or to shop. Children on their way home from school ran through the main street and were met by mothers and grandmothers.

In silence too they reached the silver-grey Ferrari and got in it. Down the winding road it swooped. Only once did Norma look back, trying to see the golden hilltop town through the back window, but all she could see was a dark smudge against the sky.

Shadows lengthened and lights began to twinkle from scattered houses and villages. By the time they reached the bridge to cross over the Arno to Florence the wide-spread city was ablaze with many lights and the huge dome of the Cathedral was a dark mysterious shape silhouetted against a lingering pale streak in the night sky.

The car stopped in the small *piazza* in front of the hotel. Roberto switched off the engine and the headlamps.

'I won't come in with you,' he said coolly. 'The sooner I leave here the sooner I'll get to Rome.'

Disappointment flooded through her. All the way back from San Gimignano she had indulged in a crazy fantasy. She had hoped he would drive on through Florence and out along the road to Rome. She had hoped he would ignore her refusal to go back to Rome with him and live with him there and that he would play the arrogant demanding lover, carry her off to his house and imprison her there; imprison her with his love.

But the beautiful capsule of time in which she had been trapped with him was over, and she had destroyed it herself by her refusal to do as he wished. Now the pressure of their everyday lives, their pasts, their futures, crowded into their minds, bringing them down to reality from the high tower of romance which they had visited so briefly together.

'The letters,' she said.

'What about them?'

'You'll have to send them to me.' She groped in her handbag for a business card. 'Roy said I was to take them back to him if I couldn't deliver them to the person who had written them.' She

scribbled the address of her flat in London on the
back of the card, peering at it by the light slanting
into the car from a street lamp. She turned to him
and offered him the card. 'There is my business
address and also the address of my flat,' she said.
'You can send the letters to either and I'll return
them to him.'

Roberto took the card from her and slipped it
in a pocket. The light from the street lamp turned
his face into a caricature of its reality. The long
dark eyes seemed longer and darker. He looked
even more secretive and slightly wicked, like one
of the men who might have been hired by the
Medici family, the rulers of Florence, and who
had gone about in cloaks and with daggers,
slipping at night through the twisting narrow
streets to spy on and perhaps kill any of the
Medicis' enemies.

'I won't be sending any letters to you,' he said.

'But Roy wants to have them for the biography
of my mother he's going to write.'

'He can't use them without my permission,' he
retorted. 'And now I have them I'll keep them.'
He paused, then went on in a different voice, a
voice that softened and purred as he leaned
towards her, 'Do you realise that if Maria hadn't
kept the letters and hadn't left instructions for
them to be returned, you and I would never have
met?' He paused again, his lips hardly an inch
from hers, then murmured, ' "*Never met—or
never parted, We had ne'er been brokenhearted*", to
quote another of your British poets. And so
goodbye, sweet Norma.'

His lips claimed hers in another tantalising kiss
that left her hungry for more. Suppressing a

longing to fling her arms about him and shout out that she didn't want to leave him, she turned away from him. Blindly she fumbled for the lever of the door, opened it and almost fell out of the car on to the pavement, unable to say goodbye to him because her throat was choked with tears.

The car door slammed shut, the engine started up. The car moved away. Norma hurried towards the hotel entrance and into the foyer to the desk to ask for her room key.

'Signorina Seton?' asked the handsome smartly dressed desk clerk, his dark Italian glance roving curiously over her face.

'Yes.'

'There is a message for you.' He gave her a folded piece of paper with her key. She thanked him and made for the elevators.

In the elevator she was glad she was alone and leaned against the wall, her eyes closed. She felt sick with disappointment, sick and ready to die because Roberto had said goodbye to her again. The words he had quoted and which she recognised as being from a love-poem by Robert Burns whispered through her mind over and over again. '*Never met—or never parted.*' Where had she read them recently? And why had he quoted them?

At last she reached her room. She closed the door and went over to the narrow window to close the indoor shutters. The lamps, red-shaded, cast warm light over the heavy dark furniture, the cream walls and the heavy ceiling beams. She sat down in an armchair and opened the note. It informed her that a Signor Aubrey Brenton had called from Milan and had left a message saying he would see her tomorrow afternoon at the Hilton Hotel, in Milan.

Aubrey in Milan? Norma re-read the message and waited for some response to it from inside herself, some feeling of joy. But nothing happened. She didn't care if Aubrey was going to be in Milan or not. She didn't care if she never saw Aubrey again. She could only think of Roberto and wish she had had the courage to toss caution to the winds to go with him, back to Rome to live with him there.

All through the long night she thought about him and wished she had gone with him to live with him in the house where his father and her mother had been lovers for a while and where he and she had been lovers for a night. Now that she knew that his father had been separated from his mother, possibly divorced from her, she could understand why the older Cortelli had fallen in love with his young and beautiful pupil.

Oh, if only Cortelli Senior hadn't written those letters to Maria! If only her mother hadn't left instructions for them to be returned to the author of them and Roy hadn't asked her to take them to the house on the Via Scipione she would never have met Roberto and she wouldn't be lying here in torment, wishing she had gone with him.

'Never met—or never parted.' Oh God, why had he quoted those words? They were so true. If he and she had never met they wouldn't have parted and she would not have been brokenhearted. Why had he said them? To make sure she would suffer through the night? As a sort of subtle revenge because she had refused to go with him to Rome?

Supposing she had given in to desire and had let her emotions rule her for once, how long would the affair have lasted? Not long, she guessed. She was probably one of several women Roberto had loved and had asked to live with him. It might have lasted a year at the most. Passionate pleasure such as they had experienced with each other was usually shortlived, so she had read. Sometimes it lasted only a few hours or days, and if you tried to make it last longer it only died down. And she would hate that. She wouldn't be able to bear seeing the flame of Roberto's present desire for her die down slowly and go out. Better to go on with her career and to marry Aubrey, who even if he wasn't passionate, couldn't hurt her as Roberto could and already had.

When sunrise came she dragged herself wearily from the bed, remembering how joyous waking up had been the previous morning, how she and Roberto had played together in the shower. Her mind was numb, beyond pain. She dressed, re-packed her case and left the room. She breakfasted on coffee and a croissant, looking out of a wide window of the restaurant at the sunlight shining on the red dome of the Cathedral making it look as if it were on fire. She checked out at the desk and went by taxi to the station. There she booked a seat on the train to Milan.

By ten o'clock she was seated in the corner of a compartment staring dully out of the window at tall cypress trees, glowing oaks and silvery olive trees, and was wishing over and over again that she could have yesterday and Roberto back again.

CHAPTER SIX

NORMA had hardly checked into her room at the Hilton Hotel in Milan when the phone rang. Guessing it was Aubrey calling to find out if she had arrived—although she suspected he would ask at the desk if she had before calling her room—she let it ring three times before lifting the receiver.

'Norma?' He didn't wait for her to say hello. 'Glad you're here at last. Were you surprised to get my message in Florence?'

He sounded as always, his tone of voice cool and clear yet somehow smug, as if he was pleased with himself for having surprised her.

'Yes, I was,' she replied cautiously.

'Actually I tried to get in touch with you at the hotel you were supposed to be staying in in Venice, but when I was told you weren't there I spoke to Melinda and she said you'd stayed behind in Florence. Why did you do that?'

'I . . . I had something I wanted to do there. There was so much to see in Florence and we didn't have much time to visit the galleries. You've been there, so you know what it's like.'

'Yes, I know.' Now he sounded understanding and she relaxed. 'Look,' he went on, 'if you're not too tired after the journey why don't we meet— say in half an hour—for a drink in the bar and we can compare notes about Florence?' It was what he liked to do most, to talk about art and books and the places he had visited, the museums and galleries he was knowledgeable about, and usually she liked listening to him and had learned much from him.

'All right, I'll see you in half an hour in the bar,' she said, and rang off.

Exactly half an hour later she walked into the bar lounge which was just off the foyer and furnished like the lounge in an English inn, with prints of English hunting scenes on the wall. Judging by the sound of the voices of the people sitting about, English was the language spoken in there, mostly with an American accent.

Aubrey was already there, seated in a corner. Impeccable as ever, his light brown hair smoothly brushed, his square face slightly pinkish and shining, his hazel eyes assessing her as she walked towards him, he stood up as she approached the round table and indicated that she should sit on the curved, padded seat beside him. When she sat down he leaned towards her as if to kiss her and Norma turned her head quickly, presenting her cheek to him, her heart sinking a little. She hoped he hadn't come to Milan to make love with her. At the moment she felt she couldn't make love with any man other than Roberto. After Roberto ... She dragged her thoughts back from the way they were going. Was her life going to be like this forever more? Would it be divided in her mind into three sections: Before Roberto. Roberto. And after Roberto?

'You're tired,' Aubrey stated as if he had just made an important discovery. 'You've overdone things in Florence, I expect. Too much walking and standing. Melinda tells me you did the Uffizi with her, so where did you go yesterday?'

'Oh, Melinda is here already?' she asked, avoiding his question.

'I believe she came in by bus from Venice at lunchtime. She's in her room resting now,' he said rather distantly. 'She told me about the Uffizi when I called her in Venice to ask her where you were.' He frowned, his thin lips pursing in a rather petulant way that they did when he was irritated. 'She also told me that you went off by yourself in Rome and stayed out all Monday night.' He gave her an underbrowed glance. 'Is that true?'

Norma was saved from answering by the arrival of a waiter who came to take orders for their drinks. She chose a Campari soda and so did Aubrey, and the waiter went away.

'Yes, it's true,' she replied calmly, although her heart had begun to beat faster than usual as it always did when she was forced to prevaricate. 'I didn't stay the night at the hotel. I stayed at the home of a . . . a friend. A friend of my mother's.'

'Oh?' His thin fair eyebrows went up in surprise. 'You didn't tell me you were going to call on anyone in Rome before you left?'

'If you care to remember, Aubrey,' she said with some asperity, 'you weren't in London when I left. You were in Germany, and I didn't know I would be going to call on Signor Cortelli until just before I left. Roy asked me to take something to him; something my mother had asked should be returned to him when she died. Signor Cortelli invited me to dinner and asked me to stay the night, so I did. That's all.'

'Cortelli.' He was frowning again. 'The name is familiar.'

'He was an opera singer and taught my mother. I have some of her records with him singing and I've played them to you. Remember? The arias from *Il Trovatore* and *La Bohème* that I have?'

'Ah yes,' he nodded. 'Very fine, both of them. He had a singularly sensuous tone for a tenor. His lower range was very . . .' He paused and smiled slightly. 'If you don't mind me using the word . . . it's the only one I can think of to convey the velvety suggestive tone he was able to give his low notes . . . but they were sexy, very sexy.'

'I know what you mean,' said Norma, nodding, thinking not of Cortelli Senior's lower range but of Roberto's.

'So that must have been very interesting for you, to meet him,' Aubrey continued smoothly after sipping some of his Campari. He flicked her another underbrowed glance. 'Did you meet his son, too? He is, I believe, making quite a name for himself as a film director.'

She took quite a long drink of her Campari, feeling her nerves twang in reaction to his question. How should she answer? How much had Melinda, damn her for being a gossip, told him?

'Yes, I met him,' she replied coolly. 'He came to the hotel. I think Melinda saw him meeting me when he came to take me to dinner.' She paused, then added quickly, changing the direction of the conversation, asking him a question for a change, 'When did you arrive in Milan? Yesterday?'

'No, today. Flew here this morning.' Aubrey frowned at his drink. 'To tell the truth, Norma,

when I called Venice and you weren't there I was
. . . well, to put it mildly, upset.'

'Why?' She was surprised.

'I . . . I thought I knew where you were. I
thought you would be in Venice because you had
said you'd be going there after finishing the
business in Florence. You gave me the dates and
the names and telephone numbers of all the
hotels you'd be staying in, if you remember, so I
thought I knew where you were. It was very
disturbing to find that you weren't where I
expected you to be. Extremely so. And that's why
I decided to come to Milan today.'

'To make sure I would be where you expected
me to be today, tonight and tomorrow, I
suppose,' she said dryly.

'Partly. I also have some business to do at our
Italian office here tomorrow. I want to discuss
something with one of our translators.' He drank
some more Campari and then turned to her, his
expression very serious. 'I also want an answer,
Norma, to my proposal. You said you'd let me
know when this trip is over, but I find I can't
wait. I have to be sure of you, and the only way I
can be sure of you is for us to be married. I think
if we're married I'll know where you are when
you go away. I'll know I can trust you not to
become involved with someone else. Do you
understand what I'm getting at?'

'Yes, I think I do. You want to be sure I'll
come back to you when I've been away and that
I'll be there when you return when you've been
away. It's called commitment and it's what
marriage is all about; at least, it was what my
mother's marriage to Roy was all about.'

'You've expressed it very well. That's exactly what I mean. I guess you must have been thinking about my proposal while you've been here in Italy, and that gives me hope,' said Aubrey in his precise way. 'So, are you ready to give me an answer?'

Norma studied his face intently—and had a strange experience. While she looked at him it seemed to her that his face wavered and crumpled and its place was taken by a darker face with sculptured classical features and long narrow eyes that slanted a glance in her direction; a glance that seemed to say: *I know many lovely things about you, things you don't know about yourself, things that give me a secret pleasure.*

She blinked and looked away quickly, her heart hammering, her pulses throbbing.

'Norma, what's the matter?' Aubrey sounded concerned.

'Nothing. Why do you ask?' she demanded, looking back at him.

'Well, quite honestly, you look as if you've seen a ghost,' he said with a little laugh. 'That's a terrible cliché, I know, like saying Cortelli's voice was sexy, but you really looked frightened and went white.' He touched his clean-shaven face with an exploring hand. 'I hope I didn't frighten you.'

'No, of course not.' She tried to smile at him reassuringly.

'Then it's the thought of marriage to me,' he suggested, and did something that was out of character because he was not normally demonstrative. He reached out and took hold of one of her hands. 'I realise it's a big and serious step for you to take at this point in time when you're on your way to being successful in your career,' he said earnestly. 'I also realise that there's quite a difference in our ages—I shall be forty next month. But I really believe we could make quite a go of it, Norma. We're neither of us possessive or demanding by nature. We both know how to live and let live. We could have a pleasant time together.'

'I know that, Aubrey . . . and believe me, I'm tempted. If I married you I'd feel so safe . . .' Her voice trailed away. Safe from falling in love. *You are not so unlike Maria as I had thought. She was also afraid of love.* Roberto's voice sounded mocking in her ears. Had that been true of her mother? Had she run away from Roberto's father, afraid of his love, afraid of the passion he had expressed so exquisitely in his letters? Had Maria run away from the dark and dangerous depths of his passion to the safety and serenity of marriage to Roy?

'It touches me to hear you say you feel safe with me,' Aubrey was saying. 'So may I announce our engagement as soon as we get back to London? I'd have liked us to have been married as soon as possible, but I realise we have to think of others too. An engagement to marry is the first step to commitment and would certainly relieve me from the anxiety I feel every time you go away on your own. You see, Norma, I want to feel safe too, safe in the knowledge that one day you'll be my wife.'

It was the nearest he had ever come to showing possessiveness and for a few moments she resented it. Then she thought again of Roberto and the power of his passion. If she agreed to an engagement she would be safe from that power when she came to Rome again, and she would be coming back to Italy in February to supervise the arrangements for the promotion of Jeremy Jenson's books published for the first time in Italian by Brenton & Humbolt.

'Yes, I think it would be a good idea to announce our engagement,' she said. 'And perhaps we could be married at Easter? The flowers are so lovely then.'

'Easter would do very well,' he replied, sitting back and letting go of her hand as he looked past her. 'Here's Melinda. Shall we tell her?' he asked.

'If you want to,' she said. Maybe if Melinda knew that they were engaged she would stop gossiping.

'I want to,' said Aubrey. He continued to stare past her at Melinda and there was an expression of smug satisfaction on his voice. 'Oh, yes, I want to very much. I want to see her face when she knows. You see, she's been saying some nasty things about you lately—little sneering innuendoes about . . . well, about your sex life. I told her she was wrong, that you're not one of those women who sleeps around. Now she'll know how I feel about you.' He rose to his feet politely and his smile at Melinda was as urbane as ever. 'Well, Melinda, how do you feel now? Headache gone?'

Anger with Melinda raging through her, boiling along her veins, Norma forced herself to be polite too and asked after Melinda's health as the other woman sat down in the chair Aubrey held for her. As always Melinda was dressed flamboyantly in a gown of wide black and blue stripes and over her shoulders she wore a black silk Italian shawl embroidered with large red cabbage roses. Her hair was swept up tightly from her neck into a chignon.

'I'm not feeling too bad now,' Melinda replied, her voice sounding a little nasal. 'I picked up a cold in Venice.' She gave Norma a knowing glance. 'So glad you were able to tear yourself away from Florence. Did your extra day come up to your expectations?'

'Yes, it did, thank you,' Norma said noncommittally. 'Did you like Venice?'

'It was all right if you like lots of water everywhere. The buildings, the Doge's Palace and St Mark's were wonderful, I admit, but I didn't really see much. It was so cold and damp, I stayed in the hotel most of the time— fortunately it had been modernised and was extremely comfortable.' Melinda turned to Aubrey. 'I feel I'd have got much more out of the place if I'd been with someone who knows it well, like you do, Aubrey.'

'I really don't know why you went,' he retorted. 'You couldn't possibly enjoy Venice to its fullest extent on such a short visit. Why, you were there only for an afternoon and one night. It would have been better if you'd stayed in Florence and seen more there.'

'Ah, but you see, I didn't want to be *de trop*, as the French so wittily put it,' drawled Melinda with a sly glance at Norma. 'Or as we English put it, two's company and three's a crowd. Don't you agree, Norma?'

'I really don't know what you're talking about,' said Norma sharply. Surely Melinda didn't know

Roberto had come to her in Florence? How could she know? She glanced at Aubrey. He was looking at her and frowning again, so she said quickly and meaningfully, 'Aubrey and I have something to tell you, don't we, darling?'

His eyebrows went up in surprise at the endearment, but he caught on and nodded, smiling rather complacently.

'Yes, we have. And tonight is going to be a celebration, so I hope you feel well enough to come to dinner with us, Melinda. Norma and I are engaged to be married.'

The waiter came with the tray of drinks Aubrey had ordered, and while he set them down Norma watched Melinda from under her lashes. Was her imagination playing tricks, or had the other woman gone very pale? Difficult to tell, since Melinda wore so much make-up and had her head tipped down as she looked in her handbag for her cigarettes. The waiter went away.

'Then I suppose congratulations are in order,' Melinda said coolly when she had found her cigarettes and had put them down with her lighter on the table beside her drink. She lifted her glass. 'Best wishes to you both,' she said rather indifferently. 'I hope you'll invite me to the wedding. Have you set the date yet?'

'Norma would like to be married at Easter,' said Aubrey.

'But that's months away!' exclaimed Melinda, giving Norma another knowing, sly glance. 'I'd have thought you'd have wanted to do it at Christmas, if not before, just to be on the safe side.'

YOUR
DREAMS
CAN
COME
TRUE
H•A•R•L•E•Q•U•I•N
FIRST•CLASS
Sweepstakes
AIR FRANCE
Enter and you can win a
ROLLS-ROYCE™
TRIP TO PARIS
MINK COAT

O EXPERIENCE A WORLD OF ROMANCE.

How to Enter Sweepstakes & How to get 4 FREE BOOKS, A FREE TOTE BAG and A BONUS MYSTERY GIFT.

1. Check ONLY ONE OPTION BELOW.
2. Detach Official Entry Form and affix proper postage.
3. Mail Sweepstakes Entry Form before the deadline date in the rules.

H·A·R·L·E·Q·U·I·N

FIRST·CLASS
Sweepstakes

OFFICIAL ENTRY FORM

Check one:

☐ Yes. Enter me in the Harlequin First Class Sweepstakes and send me 4 FREE HARLEQUIN PRESENTS® novels plus a FREE Tote Bag and a BONUS Mystery Gift. Then send me 8 brand new HARLEQUIN PRESENTS® novels every month as they come off the presses. Bill me at the low price of $1.75 each (a savings of $0.20 off the retail price). There are no shipping, handling or other hidden charges. I understand that the 4 Free Books, Tote Bag and Mystery Gift are mine to keep with <u>no obligation to buy</u>.

☐ No. I don't want to receive the Four Free HARLEQUIN PRESENTS® novels, a Free Tote Bag and a Bonus Gift. However, I <u>do</u> wish to enter the sweepstakes. Please notify me if I win.

See back of book for official rules and regulations.   108–CIP–CAJ4
Detach, affix postage and mail Official Entry Form today!

FIRST NAME_____ LAST NAME_____
                              (Please Print)

ADDRESS_____APT._____

CITY_____

PROV./STATE_____ POSTAL CODE/ZIP_____
"Subscription Offer limited to one per household and not valid to current Harlequin Presents® subscribers. Prices subject to change."

ENTER THE H·A·R·L·E·Q·U·I·N·
FIRST·CLASS *Sweepstakes*

Detach, Affix Postage and Mail Today!

Harlequin First Class Sweepstakes
P.O. Box 52010
Phoenix, AZ 85072-9987

Put stamp here.
The Post Office
will not
deliver mail
without postage.

What on earth was Melinda implying? Norma's thoughts raced as she tried to plumb the murky depths of the other woman's mind.

'No, we couldn't possibly do it sooner,' Aubrey was saying practically. 'I'm off to the States and Canada next week for board meetings with the directors of our affiliates over there, and after Christmas I'll be going to Australia for nearly a month, getting back just in time for the Italian junket.' He smiled in a rather self-deprecatory way. 'Sorry to have to drag you two both back to business, but I would like to know how you got on in Rome and Florence. Is everything fixed up there? Did you find people co-operative?'

From then on there was no more talk about personal affairs as Norma and Melinda filled Aubrey in on the details of the arrangements they had made in Rome and Florence and went on to discuss what they intended to do in Milan the next day. Aubrey had already arranged for them to dine in the Hilton's restaurant with Giovanni Palmieri, the manager of Brenton & Humbolt's Milan office, and his wife, but Melinda reluctantly declined the invitation, saying she would prefer to go to bed and nurse her cold.

The evening passed pleasantly enough, with good food, champagne and music, and Norma received a promise from Signor Palmieri that he would personally escort her to La Scala Theatre during the next afternoon.

'The season of opera does not start until the first week of December, so unfortunately I cannot arrange for you to see an opera,' he explained. 'But you can see the auditorium and the stage and also visit the museum where, if my memory serves me correctly, you will find a photograph of your mother amongst the photographs of Maria Callasand other famous prima donnas.'

And so it happened, and the next afternoon, after she and Melinda had finished discussions with the manager of the Hilton Hotel, various members of the media, florists and booksellers, Giovanni appeared and drove her in his own car to the theatre, carefully reconstructed after the second world war to look exactly like the original building.

From a crimson-walled box on the third tier of boxes in the auditorium Norma looked down to the stage where so many great singers had sung and thought of her mother. On the stage a set was being constructed—a circular flight of steps against a background of a Chinese temple with its curved roofs.

'The set is for *Turandot* by Puccini,' Giovanni explained. 'It is being staged and directed by Franco Zeffirelli. You have heard of him, perhaps? He has made films of operas and has directed many of them.'

'Yes, I have. My mother once sang *Turandot* in this theatre,' said Norma. 'I remember her telling me how wonderful it was to sing before the audience in La Scala—and yet how frightening too, because if you didn't sing well they soon let you know about it by booing and throwing things at you.'

'That is true,' said Giovanni, laughing. 'We Italians are very particular about how an opera is sung and performed, and we believe that no foreigner can do our home-made operas by Verdi Rossini and Puccini justice. Tell me, was your mother booed?'

'Oh, no. They threw flowers.'

'Then she must have performed to their satisfaction.'

'Well, she wasn't entirely foreign,' explained Norma. 'She was half Italian. Can we go to the museum now? I would like to see her photograph.'

One last look at the gold and crimson auditorium with its ornate decorations and huge chandelier and then they left the box to walk to the museum rooms, where mementoes of the great Italian opera composers had been collected. Busts and paintings and photographs of Donizetti, Rossini, Bellini and Verdi were everywhere, and there was actually a whole room devoted to Verdi which included the piano on which he had composed so many of his famous arias.

The photograph of Maria Crossley was only small and could have easily been overlooked among those of other more famous prima donnas. It showed Maria in the part of Norma, the part she had been so fond of singing. Near the photographs of the prima donnas were other photographs of several male singers, including one of Roberto Cortelli. Norma lingered in front of it for a while, trying to find in the rather sad face a resemblance to Roberto and also trying to find a spark of passion, the passion that had been expressed in his letters to Maria, but she saw only sadness.

Next day, exactly a week after she had flown to Rome, she flew back to London with Aubrey and Melinda. Looking down at the peaks of the Alps, dark and bare, poking up through the scarves of whitish-grey clouds swirling about them, she thought of the last time she had seen them the previous Sunday morning.

That had been before she had met Roberto. That had been when she had been in control of her destiny, a free woman, free to make choices for herself. Now she was different. In one short week she had lost her heart to one man and had promised to marry another.

It was raining when they landed at Heathrow, and after ordering them to stay near the exit doors of the terminal building where they had deplaned, Aubrey went off to find his car.

'I take it you haven't told him about your little fling in Rome and Florence with Roberto Cortelli,' drawled Melinda as she lit a cigarette. It was the first time Norma had been alone with the other woman since they had been in Florence. 'I gather you're going to keep him in the dark about your secret affair with another man.'

'What other man have I had an affair with?' queried Norma, not looking at Melinda. This time she mustn't make the mistake she had made in the train going to Florence. She must avoid exclaiming: *How do you know his name? How do you know he came to Florence?* She must play it cool and not betray herself any more to this woman who for some reason wished to destroy her friendship with Aubrey.

'With Cortelli, of course. I saw him in the hotel in Florence—I was in the foyer. I'd gone down to see if I could get a book about the galleries in Florence before leaving from the desk and I saw him walk in and go straight to the elevators. I changed my mind about the book and got in the same elevator as him. He got out at the floor your room was on. I could only assume he had come to see you and that he spent the night with you, and the next day. Naturally when Aubrey called me in Venice asking where you were I told him about your rendezvous with Cortelli.'

'Why? Why did you tell him?' demanded Norma, swinging round to face the other woman. 'Why should you interfere?'

'Because I'm very fond of Aubrey and I think he ought to know about you. I think he ought to know just what a little cheat you are,' retorted Melinda, her lips thinning and her eyes glittering with hostility. 'Oh, we all know at Brenton & Humbolt how besotted Aubrey is about you, and we all know how you've used your friendship with him to get the contract for the Italian promotion for Bright & Stevens. I wouldn't be at all surprised if now that you've hooked him and are engaged to him you'll be putting pressure on him to get rid of me so that you can take over the PR Directorship at Brenton's!'

Norma discovered she was trembling with rage. Never had she been spoken to so spitefully, and never had she considered how her friendship with Aubrey might have looked to the people who worked for him before.

'I ... I ... haven't used Aubrey,' she was stammering in self-defence when the exit doors opened and he came in.

'Come on, hurry up,' he ordered. 'I can't stay long outside.'

He picked up some cases and went outside, Norma and Melinda following with the rest of the luggage.

On the way into London they dropped

Melinda off in Chelsea, then drove straight to Norma's flat. Much to her relief Aubrey didn't stay when he had seen her into the flat.

'I have to go down to see my mother this evening at Tonbridge,' he explained, 'and I'll be staying the night there. I'll arrange for the announcement of our engagement to appear in all the usual newspapers this week. If that's all right with you?'

'Aubrey ... there's something I should tell you, something we should discuss, before ... before you do that. When you know you might not want to ... to, well you might not want to be engaged to me,' she said.

'Not, now darling,' he said. 'I haven't time. Mother is expecting me for dinner and before I set off I'd like to call in at my flat, leave my cases there and change my clothes.' Bending his head, he kissed her on the cheek because she turned her head quickly to avoid his lips. 'And I really don't want to know,' he said in a whisper. 'I'd rather not know because I want to be engaged to you. I'll be back tomorrow. I'll call you at your office and perhaps we could go and see Roy in the evening, give him our news. 'Bye for now.'

He left, closing the door of the flat behind him. Norma looked around at the familiar room that had been home to her ever since she had gone to work for Bright & Stevens and thought of the house on the Via Scipione. This time last week she had been there and Roberto had taken her mother's letters from her and then had kissed her, and his kiss had changed her from a woman in control of her own destiny into a woman ruled by her emotions, her attraction to him.

The letters—she must tell Roy what had happened to them. She must talk to Roy. There would be comfort in talking to him. She sat down and drew the telephone towards her, dialling his number quickly. He was at home and pleased to hear from her, and after the usual questions concerning the weather in Italy and had she liked Rome and Florence he went straight to the point and asked her if she had found Roberto Cortelli.

'I found his son,' she said. 'He's Roberto Cortelli, too, and he lives in the house on the Via Scipione. He told me his father died this year, about a month before Mother did.'

'That's odd,' said Roy. 'I'd have thought his death would have been announced in our papers. But then maybe he wasn't all that well known in this country and so his death wasn't considered newsworthy. I suppose you've brought the letters back.'

'No, I haven't. He . . . the son . . . kept them. I left my address with him and asked him to send them to me, but he said he wouldn't be returning them. He also said you couldn't use them without his permission.'

'Oh, well. I can't blame him for that,' said Roy easily. 'That's very understandable. Maybe I'll write to him now that I know he exists. He'll probably remember your mother. Did he say he'd met her?'

'Yes, he did. He said he and she used to talk a lot to each other when she was taking lessons from his father.'

'Then he could have a lot of information about Maria and his father that should go into the biography. Yes, I think I'll write to him and ask if I can interview him. What does he do? Is he a singer too?'

'No, he's a film director. He said he hopes one day to make a film about his father's life as an opera singer.'

'Did you like him?'

'Yes . . . yes, I did,' admitted Norma.

'Good. So what other news have you?'

'Aubrey came to Milan . . . and we got engaged. It'll be in the papers this week and we're going to come and see you tomorrow evening, if that's all right.'

'I see. So you've taken the plunge, have you? When is the wedding?' Roy asked.

'Not until Easter.'

'Plenty of time for you to change your mind,' he scoffed.

'Roy, you remember when we last talked together you said that Mother had never told you anything about having an affair with another man before you and she were married but you always suspected there had been someone?'

'Yes, I remember.'

'Well, if she had told you . . . if she'd come clean and told you about Cortelli then would you still have married her?'

There was a short silence, then he said:

'What's up, Norma? Are you thinking of making a clean breast of all the affairs you've had with other men before you marry Aubrey?' Mockery lilted in his voice. 'You've had so many,' he continued laughingly.

'Just answer my question, Roy, please,' she pleaded. 'If Mother had told you she'd had a love affair with Cortelli would you have married her?'

'Yes. Yes, I would. You see, Norma, I loved her, and any love affairs she'd had before she met me didn't count with me, I didn't want to know about them. But don't tell Aubrey everything about yourself. If he loves you he doesn't want to know.'

'And you don't think I'll be cheating if I don't tell him?'

'Not at all. Do you really believe he's going to tell you about the affairs he's had with other women?—and he must have had a few. He's no chicken.'

'No, I don't believe he will—and anyway, I wouldn't want to know,' she said. 'Thanks, Roy. Thanks for the advice.'

'Going to take it?'

'Yes.'

'Well, that makes a nice change,' he mocked. 'See you tomorrow evening and we'll break out the champagne.'

CHAPTER SEVEN

AFTER the official announcement of her engagement it seemed to Norma that the weeks flew by. She was so busy at work that she hardly had time to think about her personal affairs, and sometimes she even forgot she was engaged. Only when she felt the ring that Aubrey had given her—an opal surrounded by tiny pearls—did she remember.

But if she forgot about Aubrey when she wasn't with him she didn't forget Roberto, and it was as if he wouldn't let her forget him. He was always there at the back of her mind, a dark and dangerous shadow looming across her usually sunny outlook on life, reminding her of the hours they had spent together making love and creating in her a frustration that was purely sexual, so that she spent nights of agony longing to be with him and to feel his hands and his lips guiding her over the shimmering waves of sensuality to the ecstasy of physical and spiritual union with him.

Christmas came, and she and Roy went down to Tonbridge to spend it with Aubrey's mother in the old stone manor house belonging to the Brenton family. Aubrey's two sisters were there also with their husbands and their children, and altogether it was a jolly family affair which she had enjoyed. It was obvious that Aubrey's family approved of his choice of a wife, and as a result she felt safe and comfortable with them.

'You're so much nicer than Lucy was,' Jean,

Aubrey's youngest sister, confided to Norma when they were both taking their turn in the kitchen, preparing the evening meal on Boxing Day.

'Lucy?' queried Norma.

'Aubrey was married to her years ago. It didn't last long, only a couple of years. She just didn't fit in with the Brentons. Mother detested her and was jolly glad when Aubrey divorced Lucy. She was very flashy in her clothes and in her tastes in music and books. We could never understand why Aubrey had been attracted to her in the first place. Anyway, that was all over years ago, but we have been a bit worried about that Melinda woman who works for Brenton & Humbolt's. Another predatory type of woman, Mother says, who's had her eyes on Aubrey ever since she went to Brenton's. We're really thankful you've been around, Norma, believe me. Mother thinks very highly of you—says you've been well brought up and know how to behave. She couldn't stand the way Lucy would hold hands with Aubrey or kiss him in public. Mother doesn't approve of demonstrations of affection in public, and I don't think she knows what passion is.' Jean laughed a little self-consciously. 'We Brentons are very down-to-earth people. We don't go in for all that romantic mush.'

So she had noticed, thought Norma dryly, to herself. What would the Brentons think of her if they knew of her little affair in Rome and Florence? They would hardly approve of that. If they knew about her and Roberto they would no doubt put her in the same category as Lucy and Melinda.

The brief conversation with Jean gave her much food for thought. She wondered why Aubrey had never mentioned to her that he had been married before. Not that it mattered that he had, she added hurriedly. What he and she had done before they had met and had decided to become engaged was unimportant. Still, the knowledge that he had been married to an 'unsuitable' woman in Mrs Brenton's view did give him a new dimension. He was not so perfect as he made out to be. He could make mistakes, too.

And then there was the remark about Melinda having had her eye on Aubrey. That gave her a new insight into Melinda's behaviour in Italy and her spiteful remarks. Those remarks had been made out of jealousy. Melinda was jealous of her, Melinda wanted Aubrey for herself and was not above pointing out to him that the woman he had chosen to marry was not what she seemed to be.

Perhaps it would be wise to tell Aubrey what had happened in Rome between herself and Roberto, and then he could never accuse her of having been a cheat if he found out from someone else. The trouble was she didn't want to tell him—not because she was afraid he might break off their engagement if he knew but because she wanted to keep those hours spent with Roberto to herself. They were her secret pleasure that she hugged to herself and mulled over in the privacy of her flat. They were not to be destroyed or desecrated by sharing them with Aubrey or anyone else. They belonged only to her and Roberto.

The New Year came in, cold and inclined to be

foggy. Aubrey was full of his plans for his trip to Australia.

'Three whole weeks in summer-time and then straight to Rome,' he said to her as he drove out to Barnes one evening. Roy had invited them both out to see him to meet someone he had staying with him, he had said rather mysteriously when he had phoned Norma. 'I wish you were coming with me,' Aubrey went on. 'But then I know you can't because you'll be busy finalising the arrangements for the Italian trip.'

'Will you return to London before going to Rome?' asked Norma.

'If I have time. If I haven't I'll fly straight to Rome from New Zealand. I'll let you know, of course. I'll be keeping in touch with Melinda at Brenton's every day by Telex and she'll let you know of any change in my plans.'

Roy greeted them warmly when they arrived and led them both into the living room, where lights were blazing. As they followed him into the room a man who had been lounging in one of the armchairs looking at a book rose to his feet politely.

One glance at him and Norma felt the blood drain from her face and her nerves twang. It took her all her self-control not to go up to him and fling her arms about him. In the next instant it was taking all her control not to rush out of the room and from the house.

Tall and black-haired, he was casually dressed in a colourful sweater and dark pants, and he was looking right at her as if he knew things about her she didn't know. He was looking at her as if he guessed at the turmoil of her emotions on seeing him so unexpectedly and was secretly amused.

'You remember Roberto Cortelli, Norma. You and he met in Rome in November when you were on a little errand for me.' Roy was being the jovial host and at the same time making an explanation for Aubrey.

Now the blood was surging back into her face, making her cheeks burn. She swallowed hard, very aware that all three men were watching her.

'Yes, of course I remember,' she said, trying to sound welcoming and cheerful. 'How are you, Signor Cortelli?'

She greeted him formally, thinking that would put to rest any suspicions Aubrey might have, and held out her right hand. His lips curling in a slightly sardonic smile, Roberto shook her hand.

'I am very well, thank you, *Miss* Seton,' he said. His eyes were dancing now with unholy mirth. He knew all about her discomfiture at having to meet him in front of Aubrey.

'And this is Aubrey Brenton, manager of marketing for Brenton & Humbolt's the publishers and also Norma's fiancé,' continued Roy. 'Aubrey, I'd like you to meet Roberto Cortelli, son of my late wife's singing teacher, the famous Italian tenor. Roberto is also a film director and is interested in meeting Jeremy Jenson.'

'Nice to meet you, Cortelli.' Aubrey was at his most urbane, as he shook hands with Roberto. 'Well, I think a meeting with Jeremy can be easily arranged for you. Will you be in Rome in February?'

'Probably,' said Roberto.

'Then Norma here can issue an invitation to

you to the luncheon we're putting on at the Excelsior Hotel to launch our new Italian line. We're translating all our best-sellers into Italian and publishing them in Italy in association with the Palmieri publishing company in Milan. It's a new venture and we're very excited about it. Jeremy is going to kick off for us by being at the luncheons in Rome, Florence and Milan and signing copies of his first book in translation.' He glanced at Norma, bestowing on her one of his most approving glances. 'Norma here set up the arrangements for everything when she was over in Italy. But perhaps you already know that, since she met you then.'

'Yes, she did tell me about it,' Roberto grinned at Norma mischievously. 'We had some very interesting conversations, didn't we, *Miss Seton?*'

He was a devil in the guise of a handsome man, come to torment her. She could barely nod in agreement, she was so angry with him, and turned blindly to Roy.

'Can I help you fix something for us all to drink?' she asked, trying to convey to him by the way she looked at him that she had to get out of the room immediately.

'All right,' he agreed. 'Excuse us for a minute, gentlemen,' he said to the others. 'Just make yourself at home. The usual for you, I expect, Aubrey? Gin and tonic? What about you, Roberto?'

Roberto chose Scotch on the rocks and he and Aubrey both sat down, Aubrey continuing to talk as usual, nineteen to the dozen, about Jeremy Jenson's books.

In the kitchen Norma turned fiercely on Roy.

'Why didn't you tell me Roberto would be here?'

'Oh, I just thought it would make it more interesting if you didn't know, give you a little surprise,' he said, reaching into a cupboard for glasses. 'What would you like to drink?'

'Oh, anything. It doesn't matter. Orange juice will do,' she snapped irritably. 'Why is he here?'

'I told you I was going to write to him. I did, and he came here in answer to my letter. I'm very glad he has come—I've learned a lot from him already . . .' he broke off and gave her a wary glance, then added, 'About Maria and about the letters.' He dropped ice-cubes into a glass tumbler and poured Scotch over them. 'Why are you frightened of him?' he asked almost casually.

'I . . . I'm not,' she gasped. 'I just wish you'd told me he would be here tonight, that's all.'

'If I had you wouldn't have come,' he stated flatly. 'Would you?' He gave her another glance, but this time it wasn't wary. It penetrated.

'I . . . I mightn't have come,' she parried.

'Are you in love with him?'

'Roy, this is silly! Of course I'm not.'

'Maria was,' he said matter-of-factly as he poured gin into another glass. 'The letters were his. He wrote them to her.'

'You . . . you're joking,' she whispered.

'No, I'm not.' He lifted the tray of drinks and handed it to her. 'Here, you take these in. I'll be close behind you with some nuts and titbits to eat.'

It took all her courage to return to the living room and offer drinks to the two men sitting there and sitting there sipping her orange juice, and trying to appear interested in the discussion about film and TV rights to books was one of the worst experiences she had ever known. Never had she felt so uncomfortable, and all her irritation was directed at Roy now for having placed her in such a situation.

Her glance would keep drifting to Roberto no matter how much she tried to keep it away from him. She kept catching herself staring at him openly and several times he looked right at her, not warmly or with amusement any more but with a cold glitter of hostility.

'Are you staying much longer in London?' Aubrey asked abruptly after he had finished a long speech about copyright laws.

'Until tomorrow afternoon. I leave on an evening flight for Paris,' Roberto replied.

'Then pop into Brenton & Humbolt's in the morning. I'm leaving for Australia and New Zealand the day after. We can discuss this matter of film rights to Jeremy's *War in the Sun* before you go.'

'I would like to do that. You see, it is necessary that I find another story for a film,' said Roberto. 'And I would prefer that the scene be set in Italy with cosmopolitan characters. It would have a wider appeal.'

'Oh, aren't you going to make the film of *The Celebrity*?' asked Norma, breaking her silence.

'Not at this time,' he replied. 'You see, I have not been able to find an actress suitable for the part of the heroine, so I'll postpone the making of it.' He shrugged his shoulders indifferently and turned back to ask Aubrey another question.

Norma couldn't bear to be in the room any

longer. The tension she could feel building up
between herself and Roberto was too much for
her. Springing to her feet, she muttered, 'Excuse
me,' and walked out into the hallway, not sure
where she should go and deciding in the end to
slip into Roy's study and stay there until it was
time to leave, until she could persuade Aubrey to
leave.

The study was in darkness, so she switched on
a standard lamp and wandered over to the desk to
see what Roy was working on. It looked as if he
had started collecting material together for the
biography of her mother, because several black-
bound diaries were piled up on the desk.

Were the letters there? She moved some papers
about, looking for the package of letters. Had
Roberto brought them? There was no sign of
them. Had he really written them, or had he been
pulling Roy's leg when he had told him that he
had? She picked up one of the diaries and
examined the date. Exactly eighteen years ago her
mother had written in this book when she had
been in Rome, studying with Roberto's father.

Curiously she flicked over the pages. Not many
of them were filled, but those that were bore the
dates of April and May of that year.

'The situation is becoming unbearable,' the
words caught her eye because they expressed
exactly what she had felt in the living room just
now. 'I cannot go on much longer. I will have to
go away from here or give in to my own wild
desire to make love with him as he asks.
Temptation is almost too much for me, but to
give in would be to ruin his life as well as mine. I
am too old for him.'

Chilled and repelled by what she had just read, Norma let the book drop from her hands. It was true, then. Her mother had been in love with Roberto and he with her. What was it he had said to her when they had first met in Rome and she had shown him the letters and he had talked of Maria?

'*I was eighteen. Old enough to fall in love and to make love.*'

And then there had been other hints that the letters had been written by someone other than Cortelli Senior, the knowledge of the English language and the English poets.

'Why didn't you tell me you were engaged to be married when we met in Rome?'

The sound of the deep masculine voice startled her and she looked up. Roberto had come into the room and was standing on the other side of the desk, and even though his face was in the shadow she could see the cold hostile glint of his eyes.

'Because I wasn't engaged to Aubrey when I met you,' she replied as coolly as she could, although every muscle and sinew in her body had tightened up.

'But you and he have been close friends for some time, Roy tells me, and Aubrey had asked you to marry him before you went to Rome.' As he finished speaking he moved around the end of the desk until he was beside her, then sat down on it so that he was close to her and facing her. He had only to raise a hand and he would touch her. She controlled an urge to shrink back from him in case he did attempt to touch her, because if he did she would be lost and temptation would prove to be too much for her as it had almost been too much for her mother. Her mother and Roberto! Jealousy flooded through her.

'Yes, that's true,' she retorted, tilting her chin. 'He had proposed to me. I was considering his proposal while I was in Italy.'

'So I was ... perhaps your last fling, before you settled down to a life of domestic bliss with him.' His lip curled cynically.

'Oh, no, you're not to think that,' she said urgently. 'That isn't why I ...' She broke off, unable to explain why she had stayed the night with him in Rome, refusing to admit to him that she had fallen in love with him.

'What else can I think?' he taunted. 'You are after all Maria's daughter, and she was afraid of loving me, too.'

'You ... you were too young for her. She ... she said so in her diary,' she whispered, pointing to the book she had just put down.

'So you know I wrote the letters?'

'Yes. Roy told me, in the kitchen while we were getting the drinks. Why didn't you tell me you had written them before ... before ...'

'We slept together?' he suggested softly. Norma looked at him then and couldn't look away. He was gazing at her, and hostility no longer glittered in his eyes. Their expression was warm and sensuous.

'Yes,' she whispered. She felt the power of his passion flowing out from him and swirling about her like a dark and dangerous tide.

'I didn't tell you because I guessed it would have made a difference between us,' he murmured, leaning closer to her, touching her at last by taking hold of her nearest hand and raising it to his lips. She tried to snatch her hand from his grasp, but he held it tightly after kissing it.

'Of course it would have made a difference!' she hissed at him. 'I wouldn't . . . I couldn't have . . . oh, if I'd known that you and my mother had . . . had . . .' She broke off, shuddering from head to foot with revulsion at the thought of Roberto and her mother making love together, but almost immediately that feeling was swamped by another wave of jealousy; jealousy of Maria because he had written such romantically passionate letters to her.

'But Maria and I didn't do it,' he explained gently. 'Our desire for each other was never consummated. She ran away rather than do it. She ran away to England, to you and to the safety of marriage with Roy. Just as you ran away from me in Firenze when I asked you to live with me. You ran away to the safety of marriage with Aubrey. Like mother, like daughter.'

Bitterness roughened his voice and he dropped her hand as if he disliked holding it.

'What have you done with the letters?' she added.

'I've destroyed them.'

'Oh, why?' She was surprised, and showed it in the quick glance she gave him. Although he wasn't holding her hand any more he was looking at her as if he wanted to take her there and then in Roy's study with the sound of Roy's and Aubrey's voices coming from the living room. 'No,' she whispered, backing away from him. 'Please, Roberto, don't look at me like that!'

'Like what?' he asked, stepping after her.

'As if . . . as if you want to . . . to . . .' She

backed away around the other end of the desk. He followed her and stepping around her cut off her way of retreat.

'As if I want to kiss you?' he suggested, moving in on her. 'But I do. I've been wanting to kiss you ever since you came into the other room. I'm having great difficulty in keeping my hands off you.' He smiled suddenly, a bright flash in the darkness of his face. 'It is a pity we have to meet again here, in company. Why couldn't you have chosen a bedroom to run away to, when you left the other room? You're not very good at stage management,' he scoffed.

'The letters—you haven't told me about the letters,' she whispered squeakily, trying to divert him from his intention to kiss her. 'Why did you burn them?'

'Because the person who wrote them, the young man I was then, who was in love with the romance of English poetry and in love with the idea of being in love with a woman he believed was unattainable, no longer exists. He died when he realised Maria was attainable after all.' He laughed in self-mockery. 'It didn't last long, that truly romantic first love of mine, and I have loved other women since. I have loved you.'

'No, no, you haven't—you haven't! You don't know what love is. You only play at love. If . . . if you'd loved me in Rome, in Florence, you wouldn't have asked me to live with you without marriage. You're only interested in short-term affairs, not in commitment,' Norma argued wildly in a fierce whisper. 'You . . . you only want me now, because you know you can't have me, because I . . . I'm unattainable. What happened between us is over. I'm going to marry Aubrey and . . .'

'Have you told him about us?' he put in sharply.

'No.'

'Why haven't you?'

'Why should I? Mother didn't tell Roy about you, so why should I tell Aubrey about you? She soon forgot about you, and so shall I.'

She intended to hurt him, but when she saw the wicked blaze of anger in his eyes she regretted what she had said instantly.

'Not if I can help it,' he said through set teeth, his face close to hers, his breath warm on her cheek. 'I'm going to haunt you for the rest of your life, sweet Norma.'

Against her trembling lips his were hard and brutal, ravishing the softness, blurring the shape. His sharp-edged teeth nipped her flesh painfully so that a muffled cry rose in her throat while her own teeth were pressed into the tender inside of her mouth and drew blood. And then he had gone, walking from the room as stealthily as he had come, and she was alone and shaking, feeling as if she had been violated.

Roberto wasn't in the living room when she eventually returned to that room, hoping she didn't look too pale or that her lips were too red.

'I think it's time we left, Aubrey,' she said brightly. 'You know how early I have to get up on work days.' She turned to Roy. 'Thanks for inviting us over.'

'Where's Roberto?' he asked, eyeing her suspiciously.

'I have no idea. Maybe he went to bed.'

'Now, don't forget to remind him, Roy, to call in at our offices tomorrow before he leaves for Paris,' said Aubrey as he held Norma's coat for her. 'I'm really excited by his interest in *War in the Sun*. It would make a great film in the hands of the right director, and from what I've heard about Cortelli he's well on the way to following in the footsteps of some of the great Italian film-makers of the past and of the present.'

'I'll remind him,' said Roy, opening the front door. 'Have a good time Down Under, Aubrey. I'll be in touch with you, Norma.'

'Come and have dinner with me, the day after tomorrow,' she said, pecking at his bearded cheek, 'and I'll show you how to cook another Chinese meal.'

'I'll be there,' he replied.

She and Aubrey didn't talk for a while as they drove away along lamplit streets. He broke the silence at last.

'I'm glad I've met Cortelli. It was a good idea of Roy's to ask me over to meet him. Now I can understand why Melinda is always raving about him,' he said.

'Melinda raves about Roberto?' exclaimed Norma. 'But she . . . she only saw him . . . once.' She drew back just in time from saying 'twice'.

'Twice, actually,' said Aubrey. 'She saw him in Florence too, she said. He made a big impression on her, and now I know why. He's not only a handsome man but he also possesses a powerful personality. I wouldn't like to cross him in any way. Anyway, I can understand also now why Melinda was so worried about your association with him and why she thought you and he had

something going between you. She's going to be
flabbergasted when he turns up at the office
tomorrow!' He chuckled in anticipation. 'And I
wouldn't be at all surprised if she doesn't swoon
when she sees him, she's so infatuated with him.'

Melinda infatuated with Roberto? Melinda and
Roberto. Maria and Roberto. Herself and
Roberto. God only knew how many women and
Roberto. Once more jealousy flooded through
Norma, and it stayed with her through the night
and all the next day, so that when he phoned her
the following evening the first words she spoke to
Aubrey were:

'Did Roberto Cortelli call in to see you this
morning?'

'Yes. And as I guessed, Melinda was flabbergasted to see him. He seemed quite taken with
her and took her out to lunch. Then she went to
the airport with him to see him off to Paris. By
the way, it's all fixed up for him to come to the
luncheon in Rome and we'll probably announce
then he's bought the film rights of *War in the
Sun*. Now am I going to see you this evening?
Remember I fly to Australia tomorrow.'

The night passed in torment again as Norma
thought not of Aubrey, from whom she was going
to part the next day for three whole weeks, but of
Roberto and Melinda, but she survived as she
had survived other nights of anguish, and the next
day she went with Aubrey to Heathrow to see
him off, then drove his car back to its garage at
the mews apartment where he lived in
Knightsbridge.

She was slicing vegetables when Roy arrived at
her flat, but it wasn't until they were sitting down

at the table to eat that he directed the conversation to a personal note.

'Have you told Aubrey about your affair with Roberto?' he asked, almost casually.

'What affair?' she retorted lightly.

'Now, Norma, don't try it on with me,' he rebuked her. 'You did more than pass on those letters to Roberto in Rome, and he did more than take them from you.'

'Did he tell you what happened?' she whispered. She didn't want to believe that Roberto would have told anyone of their meetings or their lovemaking. She wanted to believe that their short-lived affair was a secret he held close to his heart too.

'No. He didn't talk about you at all except to ask if he could meet you again while he was staying with me, and that's why I invited you over.' Roy sat back in his chair and regarded her with serious blue eyes while he stroked his grey beard. 'But when I told him that you were engaged I almost changed my mind about having you over—he looked as if he might commit murder! Then when you came in and saw him I realised why. It was written all over your faces how you and he felt about seeing each other again.'

'Oh, no!' she groaned, her elbows on the table, her hands clutching her hot cheeks. 'Do you think Aubrey noticed anything?'

'I don't think so. He's a bit blind, is Aubrey. I mean, he doesn't see what he doesn't want to see or what he doesn't like. Something of an escapist, I think. Are you going to tell him about your affair with Roberto before you marry him?'

'No, I'm not. It's over, and there's nothing left to tell,' said Norma firmly.

'You're quite sure?'

'Quite sure. I'm not in love with Roberto. I was for a while, but I'm not now. Since I learned about him and Mama my feelings for him have changed, and I don't care if I never see him again,' she declared emphatically.

'Really?' Roy raised his eyebrows and didn't look at all convinced, but much to her relief he changed the subject and didn't refer to Roberto again.

CHAPTER EIGHT

ON the first day of February Norma flew to Rome again. She travelled alone in advance of the rest of the people who would be involved with the book-launching luncheons. They—Melinda Morrison, Jeremy Jenson and his wife and various young men from the marketing department of Brenton & Humbolt—would be flying out tomorrow. Aubrey was already in Rome, having gone there directly from New Zealand, and would meet her off the plane. Together they would check on all the arrangements for the luncheon tomorrow and make sure that everything was in order and that there would be no last-minute hitches.

She felt calm and relaxed, sitting in the first class compartment of the plane looking down on the glittering snow-covered peaks of the Alps. Calm, cool and efficient. And that was how she wanted to feel. During the past three weeks while Aubrey had been away she had practiced positive thinking and had managed to subdue the violent emotions that Roberto Cortelli had aroused in her and had almost managed to forget him.

Almost, but not quite, for there had been moments, mostly when she had been in contact with Melinda Morrison, when he had leapt to the forefront of her mind and had blotted out everything else.

It wouldn't have happened if Melinda hadn't

persisted in talking about him every time Norma
had had to meet her to discuss the final
arrangements for the luncheon parties in Rome,
Florence and Milan; if Melinda hadn't gone on
and on about how attractive he was, about the
telephone conversations she had had with him
recently concerning the film rights for Jeremy
Jenson's book and about how much she was
looking forward to seeing him again in Rome.

'It'll make such a difference to me knowing
that he'll be at the luncheon,' Melinda had
gushed. 'To recognise someone among the sea of
strange faces.'

Norma wasn't looking forward to seeing him
again in Rome. In fact she was hoping to avoid
seeing him. Most of all she didn't want to see him
with Melinda. She wanted to avoid feeling again
that awful spiteful jealousy she experienced every
time she thought of Roberto with another
woman. The less she saw of him the better, until
she had really forgotten him—or rather, until she
could remember him without a nagging feeling of
regret, without the raw ache of desire to be with
him again in some place far away from everyday
concerns; a place where there was no past and no
future, no Maria, no Aubrey, no Melinda, and no
memory of such people; just her and Roberto,
bound together in an intimacy that kept everyone
else out, creating a world of secret pleasure where
only the two of them could live.

An announcement from the chief steward
interrupted her fantasy, bringing her back to the
plane's cabin. There was some turbulence and
the steward suggested seatbelts should be
fastened. Norma fastened hers. The man in the

next seat spoke to her, she answered, and they continued to talk for the rest of the flight and daydreams were relegated to their usual place, at the back of her mind.

It was raining when the plane landed at Rome airport and the pale fields and winter-bare trees of the surrounding countryside were blurred by a grey mistiness. After going through Customs and Immigration Norma carried her one case through to the arrivals area and looked around for Aubrey. He wasn't there, so she looked for somewhere to sit while she waited for him.

She became aware that someone was approaching her, and stiffened with incredulity. Roberto, dressed in jeans and a padded blue nylon ski jacket, was walking towards her. He came right up to her while she continued to stare foolishly at him, and took hold of her shoulders and kissed her on both cheeks.

'*Buon giorno*, Norma,' he said, looking down at her with dark secretive eyes. 'Welcome to Rome again. Let me take your case.'

'Where . . . where's Aubrey?' she managed to gasp as he took her case from her hand.

'He's sorry he couldn't come to meet you. He is tied up with some English writer who lives here in Rome and who wishes to have a book he has written published. Aubrey asked if I would come to meet you instead of him. The car is just outside.'

He turned and began to walk towards the exit doors, and Norma could do nothing else but follow him. Outside, the Ferrari looked sleek and grey. Roberto opened a door for her and after a slight hesitation, realising she was getting wet and cold as she stood there, she got into the car.

Water from large puddles spurted up from the wheels of the car as Roberto drove away from the airport. Soon they were on a wide highway dodging in and out of traffic in typical Italian style.

They were silent. For Norma the memory of their last meeting loomed large in her mind, when he had kissed her with such violence. It made her tense and speechless and she kept her head turned away from him, afraid to look at him.

Field after field flashed by. Sometimes there were houses. Tall trees without leaves seemed to droop sadly in the rain. After a while it occurred to Norma that there should be more houses, even factory buildings and apartment blocks, as they approached the outskirts of Rome. There ought to be more cars too, not fewer.

She looked away from the window beside her and through the windscreen across which the wipers were sweeping in regular rhythm. The road was climbing up a hill. There were hills all around, their lower slopes covered with vineyards. Then suddenly everything was blotted from view by swirling clouds.

'This isn't the way to Rome!' she exclaimed, turning to Roberto at last.

He didn't look at her but kept his glance on the road ahead, or all they could see of it under the rolling mist.

'I wondered when you would notice,' he drawled dryly.

'Where ... where are you going?' she whispered.

'South. To the coast.'

'But ... but I have to go to Rome, to meet

Aubrey and make sure everything is ready for the luncheon and for the arrival of the Jensons! There's so much I have to do. I haven't time to go to the coast. Roberto, please turn back at once!'

'No.'

The car reached the top of the hill and began to swoop down the other side, increasing speed as the clouds were left behind and the road forged straight ahead through a wide valley where sunlight gleamed on the walls and windows of scattered farmhouses.

'You can't do this to me. You can't!' muttered Norma furiously.

'But I am,' retorted Roberto with a laugh. 'We are going away together for this afternoon and tonight. Don't worry, I'll take you back to Rome tomorrow morning. You'll be at the Excelsior in time for the luncheon.'

'I can't go away with you. I have to meet Aubrey today and see that everything is all right at the hotel. I have to—it's part of my job.'

'To hell with your job! To hell with Aubrey too,' he growled. 'You and I need some time together—to talk. To make love. Our meeting in London was too brief. It was a disaster.'

'But you don't seem to understand . . . I . . . I don't want to have anything to do with you any more. I . . . I don't want to make love with you.'

'Methinks you do protest too much,' he misquoted mockingly. 'And you know what that means, don't you? It means that you do want to make love with me, only you won't admit it to yourself.'

'That isn't true,' she whispered. 'Oh, please stop and turn back. Please!'

'No.'

The car roared on along a road patched with sunlight and shadow past small villages surrounded by vineyards and olive groves and fruit orchards. In the distance on the far eastern side of the valley were humpy hills, and beyond them mountains on which snow glittered. On top of one of the hills a long white building glimmered.

'Where are we?' asked Norma.

'Near Cassino. That is Monte Cassino over there with the new building of the Benedictine monastery on top of it. Near here there are many cemeteries where soldiers from your country and America are buried, as well as Italians and Germans. It is a very sad place. We turn off here, for the coast.'

Off to the right they turned, over a narrow hump-back bridge and along a street of ginger-coloured houses, old houses with sagging balconies where women were hanging washing out and hens pecked for food in yards. Then the houses were gone and the road was winding before them into the sunlight that burst forth from behind the clouds making rain-wet grasses glitter. Cypress trees marched along the sides of the roads.

'You're wasting your time, you know,' said Norma, returning to the duel of wits and wills, 'carrying me off like this against my will. I can be very stubborn when I want to be . . .'

'Mulish, don't you mean?' Roberto flashed her a mocking grin.

'Ever heard of passive resistance?' she continued with a tilt of her chin, ignoring his interruption. 'Well, I'm very good at it. You'll see!'

'And I'm very good at overcoming any sort of resistance,' he retorted, his voice silky with menace. 'You'll see,' he added mockingly.

'Oh, why are you doing this? Why?' she whispered.

'Out of revenge.'

'Revenge? Revenge against whom?'

'You!'

'But I haven't done anything to you. Why would you want to be revenged on me?'

'For running away from me. For preferring to be engaged to Aubrey rather than live with me. For preferring your silly job to living with me.'

'It isn't a silly job,' she almost shouted at him, turning to glare at him. 'It's my career!'

'With a little luck you'll lose both Aubrey and your job after tonight,' he went on, giving her a wickedly glinting glance from the corner of his eye. 'And then maybe you'll not be so quick to reject any proposition I *might* make to you. You might even jump at the chance to be my mistress.'

'Never, never!' she seethed. 'Anyway, Aubrey will understand when I tell him you *forced* me to spend the night with you, when I tell him you deliberately kidnapped me!'

'What makes you think he'll be so understanding and forgiving?'

'He . . . he loves me.'

'You don't seem very sure that he does,' he scoffed.

'He asked me to marry him, didn't he? He gave me this ring.' She held up her left hand and the opal shone softly.

'I agree it wasn't nice,' he said. 'But it wasn't

unjust. It was the truth, and the truth often hurts. A guy like Aubrey couldn't get a woman like you unless he asked you to marry him. And he likes it that way. He likes to think of you as a *nice*, innocent, wholesome woman who has never looked at another man, who has never *been* with another. That's the sort of woman he believes he should have as his wife. Yet you don't love him, and by accepting his ring and his proposal you're deceiving him . . .'

'I am not,' she said stormily, glaring at him. Roberto returned her glare with a dark sceptical expression, his lips twisting, and she had to control another desire to hit him, to pummel his shoulders, his chest, anywhere, she disliked what he was saying to her so much.

'And he doesn't love you,' he said as if she hadn't interrupted him. 'This engagement between you is nothing else but a defence the two of you have built up together and behind which both of you can hide from real love.'

'It isn't, it isn't! Oh, stop it, stop, or . . . or . . . I'll hit you!' she cried furiously.

'Hit away,' he taunted, grinning at her suddenly. 'Go on, it will give me an excuse to get hold of you, shake some sense into you.'

She shifted away from him, against the door behind her.

'You wouldn't!' she fumed. 'You wouldn't dare to lay violent hands on me. And Aubrey and I aren't hiding from anything behind our engagement.'

'Oh, yes, you are. You're hiding from me because you believe I'm nothing more than an Italian philanderer, who takes what he wants from a woman and then forgets her; because you know I was once in love with your mother and that revolts you. And Aubrey is hiding behind his engagement to you from Melinda because he knows his family doesn't approve of her—she's too much like his first wife and doesn't measure up to their snobbish standards,' Roberto said jeeringly. 'As for me not laying violent hands on you . . . just try pushing me too far and you'll find out whether I'll dare or not !'

Her breast rising and falling as she breathed hard, adrenalin rushing through her nervous system, Norma stared at him in astonishment.

'Melinda?' she gasped at last. 'Are you trying to tell me that Aubrey is . . . is in love with Melinda?' She managed a scornful but rather shaky laugh. 'Oh, really, that's quite ridiculous! I've never heard anything so far-fetched in my life! You must be making it up.' She laughed again. This time she thought her scorn of him sounded convincing and she attempted a sneer, to get her revenge on him for what he had said about Aubrey only being able to get her by offering a ring and marriage. 'But then I'd forgotten you're a creator of illusion. I suppose you don't know the difference between fact and fiction.'

His eyes glittered dangerously. The slant of his black eyebrows was satanical, the curving-back of his lips threatening. Fear tripped along her nerves and behind her back she groped for the door handle, intending to fall backwards out of the car if he moved towards her with the intent to strike at her or to shake her.

'I may be a creator of illusion for the cinema,'

he said, his voice grating with anger, 'but I also am an experienced observer of human beings and their behaviour. I couldn't make films about real people if I wasn't. When I was at Brenton & Humbolt for those few hours and while I lunched with Melinda I saw enough and was told enough to convince me that Aubrey and Melinda have been in love with each other for years.'

'It isn't true. It can't be true,' Norma argued stubbornly.

'It's true,' he said. 'Time you faced up to reality of their secret affair. And never think for one moment that their affair will stop just because you and he get married. It will continue outside your marriage, because they won't be able to stop seeing each other, being with each other. They'll go on meeting, giving each other secret pleasure. And so will you and I, sweet Norma. So will you and I.'

His voice changed as he leaned close to her. Against her cheek his fingers were gentle, framing her face, tilting it up to his. She couldn't have accused him of violence even if she had wanted to. She couldn't have avoided his lips either even if she had wanted to. But she didn't want to.

There was no resistance in her to the pressure of his kiss. Her arms went up and about his neck, and at once his hands shifted away from her face and down to her zipped jacket. The zip slid open and his fingers moved assuredly under the woollen sweater she was wearing.

The shimmering waves of desire were suddenly all around her, rising higher and higher. She sank beneath them, drowned in passion. She didn't feel the hardness of the door behind her. She felt only the heat of Roberto's lips, the coolness of his fingers against her warm flesh, the roughness of his hair under her hands, and suddenly the need swelled up within her, raw and hot, to feel him inside her, lifting her once more to the paradise they had known together in Florence.

Far away, very faintly she heard the sound of a horn being blown. Roberto cursed briefly against her lips and moved away back to his seat, raking back his hair and with both hands, looking over his shoulder to peer through the rear window.

'A truck,' he muttered. 'It can't get past.' And slewing round in his seat, he started the engine and drove forward quickly.

With shaking hands Norma pulled down her sweater as she sat up straight and zipped up her jacket. Her hair was also wildly dishevelled and she searched for and found a comb in her handbag. Dragging the comb through her short locks, she took deep breaths in an attempt to control her see-sawing emotions.

It had happened to her again. This man beside her had stormed her defences and had roused her to passion again, and now she could think of nothing else but him and the longing that was leaping and hurting within her to be with him in bed, sharing secret pleasures with him.

The road straightened out before them, and she saw the sea, bands of blue and silver stretching away to a distant horizon and a village of houses strung out along the top of a cliff. Behind the Ferrari the truck groaned and rattled as Roberto drove straight into the village. He stopped the car outside a restaurant in the town *piazza* where a fountain gushed.

'Lunch first, and then we'll walk and talk,' he said, then turned to give her a mocking grin. 'Unless of course you're going to passively resist and refuse to eat, sit alone out here in the car while I indulge.'

Norma realised just how hungry she was. Breakfast courtesy of British Airways seemed a long time ago. So did her threat of passive resistance. Roberto had caught her again in his magic net. Memories of the day she had spent with him in San Gimignano thronged into her mind. This day could be another golden period of time to be treasured for ever. So why resist? Why not let herself be held captive for a few hours by passionate love?

The restaurant was owned and run by a family. The room was plainly furnished with long tables, covered with white cloths, and stacking chairs. Hand-painted murals depicted scenes of Mount Vesuvius seen from the ruins of Pompeii; a view of Capri from Naples, the houses of Sorrento sliding down cliffs to the bright blue of the Bay of Naples.

'We are not far from Naples,' said Roberto after indicating and naming the scenes. 'We should be able to see it across another bay from here.'

'What's the name of this village?' she asked.

'Sorino. It's only a small resort on the Gulf of Gaetano. I've never been here before, but Jenson mentions it in his book, so I wanted to see it and find out if it has possibilities as a locale for the film I intend to make of the book.'

'He hasn't signed the contract yet, giving you the film rights.'

'I know. But he will. He won't be able to refuse the offer I've made,' he replied confidently.

The owner of the restaurant who also acted as head waiter brought a bottle of white wine and opened it and poured two glasses then he took out his pad of paper to take their orders.

'He recommends the fried squid,' said Roberto. 'Do you like squid?'

'I've never had it. Are you going to order it?'

'Yes, since it appears to be the local delicacy. We can also have some pasta first. He suggests the *ravioli*.'

They both ordered *ravioli* to be followed by fried squid and a salad, and the owner went away. Several other people had come into the restaurant, all men in working clothes who all stared curiously at Norma.

'You would think they'd never seen a woman before,' she muttered to Roberto, who was sitting opposite to her and couldn't see the men.

'They probably haven't seen a woman like you, with red hair, wearing boy's clothes.'

'My hair isn't red ... it's ... it's strawberry blonde,' Norma retorted. 'And these aren't boy's clothes. These pants are the wrong shape for a boy.'

'Unisex clothes, then,' he drawled, smiling into her eyes. 'I love you more when you get prickly,' he added softly, reaching across and taking one of her hands in his. Still looking at her, he kissed the back of it. 'They'll stop staring now,' he added. 'Am I right?'

He was. The men all looked away from her and

started talking to each other. She nodded, feeling her cheeks glow. Would she ever get used to Roberto making love to her in public, to laying claim to her in front of others?

A young woman followed by a little girl came to the table to set knives and forks and spoons in front of them and a large basket full of hunks of white bread. Roberto spoke to the woman, who told him she was the daughter of the house and the little girl was her daughter. He asked her if she knew of a hotel or *pensione* where they could stay the night and she gave him an address. A shout from the owner of the restaurant sent the waitress scurrying off to set another table, the little girl at her heels. From the other direction from the kitchen behind the serving hatch came the sound of more shouting, this time a female voice ordering Antonio to come into the kitchen and help with the serving of the *ravioli*.

The little packets of *pasta* were stuffed with spinach and herbs and covered with cheese sauce. Norma ate all that was on her plate, hardly realising she had done so, the *pasta* was so light and fluffy. The quantity of wine sank lower and lower in the bottle and Roberto ordered another.

She found the squid, fried in crisp batter, a little rubbery, sweet to the taste, but not unpleasant, and after the salad there was fresh fruit, huge luscious yellow pears, small oranges and very ripe bananas, and glass after glass of the smooth golden wine.

'I think you're trying to make me drunk,' she accused Roberto in a whisper.

He smiled at her and her knees shook beneath the table.

'Do you still want me to take you back to Rome this afternoon?' he asked.

'If . . . if I said yes would you drive me back there?' she challenged.

'No. Not even if you pleaded with me on your knees,' he retorted softly.

'You're very cruel,' she taunted, but she didn't mean what she said.

'Only sometimes, when I want something very badly,' he murmured, his glance a mixture of arrogance and tenderness that completely defeated her. 'And I want you, today, this evening and all of tonight. Can you deny that you want me? Can you refuse to give me what I want?' His hand reached out and touched hers. 'Can you, sweet Norma? Look at me and say no. If you do I'll not insist that we stay the night here together.'

She looked at him. The moment of silence was tense as she tried hard to find the courage to refuse him. But she didn't find it. She found only the desire to be alone with him for the rest of that day and night.

'I can't. You know I can't. I can't say no,' she whispered, and saw triumph blaze briefly in his eyes.

When the meal had been paid for they walked away from the restaurant, down a narrow street lined with souvenir shops to a look-out place halfway up the cliff, and leaned against a protective wall to look across a sunlit gulf of water to the distant smudge on the horizon that Roberto told her was the city of Naples.

From the look-out they descended a flight of stone steps to a beach of firm yellow sand where fishing boats were tied up and nets were festooned between poles. Hand in hand they walked along under the sheer walls of the cliffs.

They talked very little after all. It was as if they had decided mutually that words were no longer necessary to express how they felt. But they stopped to kiss often. Sometimes the kiss was long and deeply searching, stopping only on the brink of complete physical capitulation, leaving them breathless and clinging to each other; sometimes it was a brief tantalising promise of surrender which would come later when they were completely alone in the shared privacy of a rented room.

The wind was cool but the sunshine was warm. The sand was bright yellow, the sea turquoise and silver edged with white lacy foam. They found flat stones and skimmed them over the water, each of them trying to go one better than the other. They picked up small shells and pocketed them as souvenirs of this pleasurable time spent together.

When they reached the end of the beach they turned and walked back slowly. The sun slid down the sky, the shadows lengthened. The wind grew chilly. Norma shivered, and Roberto held her closely, an arm about her waist.

Up to the *piazza* they climbed, back to the car. In a few moments they were stopping outside a house at the end of the village street on the wall of which the word *Pensione* had been painted.

The room to which they were shown was at the front of the house and overlooked the bay. Norma lingered at the long casement window looking out. The sky was flushed crimson, the clouds were violet-coloured streaked with gold. The sea was darker, a deep rich burgundy.

She felt hands on her shoulders. They slid over to her breasts. Her jacket was unzipped and slipped off her shoulders and down her arms. Lips tantalised the tender hollow at the nape of her neck and arms came around her again. Roberto's hands rested lightly for a moment at the front of her waist before his fingers slipped inside the waistband of her pants and moved downwards.

Tingling sensations shot through her nerves and she spun round swiftly to face him, breaking his hold on her. Laughingly he backed away from her to the bed and flung himself down on it on his back. His jacket was off and so was his sweater. His black collarless shirt was undone to the waist, showing olive-tinted skin criss-crossed with black hair.

He held out his arms to her invitingly and she went to him, almost running in the heat of her desire to touch him. Shamelessly she flung herself down on him, her hands seeking the buckle of his belt, then the zip of his trousers, while she kissed his cheeks, his forehead, his chin, his eyes and finally his lips.

And all the time she was kissing him she could feel desire flaming through her, lighting her up. Impatient because he wasn't doing anything but just lying there letting her undress him while his eyes danced with laughter, she began to remove her own clothes, dragging her sweater over her head.

Then he moved. While her arms were still lifted and her head was lost in the folds of the sweater he touched her, curving his hands to her silk-covered breasts,

'Oh, help me, help me to get it off,' she cried, her voice muffled by wool. 'I can't get if off!' Exquisite sensations were tingling through her from the touch of his hands and she was desperate now to be close to him.

He pulled at the sweater and it came off at last and was tossed aside. Half sitting and half lying, they faced each other, and slowly Roberto began to slide the straps of her underslip down her arms, his glance lingering on the swell of her breasts rose-coloured by the last of the sunset glow. His head tipped towards hers and their lips met. Down against the pillows they slid, and it began, the touching and the coaxing, the sighing and the whispering, the soft laughter, as they set out together again on the slow journey to paradise.

CHAPTER NINE

PALE winter sunlight gilded the formidable red
brick turrets of the San Sebastian gate next
morning when Norma and Roberto approached it
from the narrow confines of the Appian Way and
stopped at traffic lights. Two lanes of traffic
surged past them along the wide road that curved
outside the high walls which had once en-
compassed medieval Rome and had been built
outside the original walls of the ancient city.

At last the lights changed. The Ferrari shot
straight across the wide road, through the arched
gateway and into the dimness of another cobbled
road, past the remains of the original gate with its
graceful classical columns, its pale stone glimmer-
ing with a ghostly white light.

The narrow road was edged with walls
festooned with creeper. Above the walls peeped
the roofs of old villas and the tops of pine trees.
From the dimness of that road they joined a
carousel of cars going around a *piazza* and then
whizzed along the wide Via delle Terme de
Carnacalla to the Circo Massimo.

And so they crossed the city, seeming to hop
from *piazza* to *piazza*, until at last the tree-lined
Via Veneto opened up before them and they were
stopping in front of the hotel.

'I'll see you later,' said Roberto crisply as
Norma opened the door of the car to get out. He
had said little on the drive from Sorino and she

had guessed he was far away in his mind, possibly creating illusions, thinking about the film he was going to make. She took her case from the back seat of the car, said, '*Arrivederci*,' to him, then closed the door and watched the car leave the kerb and join the stream of traffic.

There was a difference, she thought, as she turned towards the glittering glass doors of the hotel, between this parting and the others. Roberto had made a sort of commitment. He had said he would see her later and he would be at the luncheon. They would meet again in a few hours, but between now and their next meeting she had to deal with Aubrey.

To her relief there was a room booked for her, and nothing was said by the desk clerk about her not having turned up the previous day. He assured her that the rest of the people from Brenton & Humbolt had arrived, said how pleased the hotel management were to have been chosen to have the luncheon in their hotel, and was generally charming. Norma went straight up to her room, unpacked, then showered quickly, noting that the guests for the luncheon would be arriving in exactly half an hour, and hoping and praying that the flowers for the tables had come, the programmes had been delivered, the tables had been set and that the chef had remembered what food was to be served.

She dressed in a golden-brown silk dress that was the colour of her eyes, made up her face, brushed her hair until it looked like a cap fashioned from red-gold silk, slipped into high-heeled tan-coloured shoes and slung the tan leather handbag she had bought at Peruzzi's in

Florence over her shoulder. After checking that she had all her notes with her she left the room and took the elevator down to the mezzanine floor.

'Norma! At last you're here!' Aubrey stepped towards her and much to her surprise kissed her on the cheek. He didn't seem to be at all put out by her late arrival. In fact he seemed to be in good spirits. He was impeccably dressed in a dark blue double-breasted suit and had a white carnation pinned to a lapel of his jacket. His fair hair was smooth, his face pink and shiny.

'Hello, Norma.' Melinda, looking as exotic as usual, in a many-coloured silk dress with an uneven hem, appeared behind him, smiling sweetly. 'Did you and Roberto have a good time?'

'Roberto?' Aubrey's hazel eyes narrowed with puzzlement.

'Roberto Cortelli. You remember, the film director who's coming to meet Jeremy today and sign the contract for the film rights,' explained Melinda.

'Yes, yes, I know who he is,' said Aubrey testily. 'But how can you have seen him already this morning, Norma? I thought you'd only just come from the airport?'

Norma's mind whirled with chaotic thoughts. There was something here that she didn't quite grasp.

'No. I arrived yesterday, on the British Airways flight that arrives just before noon. You were supposed to meet me, but you sent Roberto Cortelli instead. He told me you were busy interviewing a writer ...' Norma broke off to watch Melinda walk away to talk to someone who was sitting at a table on which copies of Jeremy Jenson's first book to be translated into Italian were piled up.

'I didn't interview any writer,' snapped Aubrey, glaring at her suspiciously. 'I had no idea you were coming yesterday. When I got here the day before yesterday there was a message waiting for me from the London office saying that Melinda would be arriving yesterday afternoon and that you wouldn't be coming until today.' His upper lip lifted in a sneer. 'You'll really have to be much more subtle if you want to cover up your secret assignations with Cortelli, you know,' he said. 'But we can't discuss that now.' He glanced at his watch. 'I'm being interviewed in a few seconds by a journalist from one of the Roman newspapers.' He turned away from her and called out to Melinda, 'Has that reporter arrived yet?'

'Yes, Aubrey. He's waiting for you in another room. This way.'

Aubrey went off with Melinda and Norma watched them go, biting her lips and frowning as she tried to guess what had happened.

It seemed that everything was ready for the luncheon. The flowers had arrived, the programmes were there. The twenty round tables in the ballroom were covered with yellow tablecloths and set with silver and glassware for ten people each. On the raised dais at the end of the room another table had been arranged for the guests of honour. The waiters were ready to serve the food. The chef had remembered to prepare chicken in a cream and wine sauce.

'The room looks pretty, doesn't it?' Melinda had entered the ballroom and she came up to

Norma. 'We have a microphone for the speakers. The TV crews have just come and are setting up their lights.' She glanced at Norma. 'You weren't missed, you know. I managed very well without you. Next time we won't bother to hire a PR company—we'll do it all ourselves.'

'I'm sorry I didn't get here yesterday,' said Norma. 'There was nothing I could do about it. Roberto wouldn't drive me here.'

'That's all right,' said Melinda cheerfully. 'I came in on a later flight to cover for you so that Aubrey wouldn't suspect anything.'

'I ... I'm afraid I don't understand what's been going on,' said Norma.

'Oh, didn't Roberto explain?' Melinda looked surprised.

'All he said was that Aubrey couldn't meet me as arranged, and then he drove me down to the coast and wouldn't bring me back until this morning.'

'He arranged it all over the phone with me, last week. He asked when you would be arriving in Rome and said he would meet you because he wanted to have some time alone with you. I suggested he did that, and then I sent a message to this hotel for Aubrey to receive, when he got here, saying you wouldn't be coming until today but I would come in your place to make sure all the details for the luncheon were in order.' Melinda smiled again. 'Don't look so bothered about it! I was only too pleased to let you and Roberto steal a few hours away on your own. It meant that I could have some time with Aubrey.' She began to walk towards the entrance to the ballroom. 'I think I hear guests arriving,' she said. 'You'd best go into the kitchen and see if the food is ready.'

'But, Melinda, why did you tell Aubrey just now that I'd been with Roberto? Why did you ask me in front of Aubrey if I'd had a good time with him if . . . if it was supposed to be a secret?' Norma demanded.

'Can't you guess, dear? I wanted to convince him once and for all what a little cheat you are.' Melinda's white teeth snapped together viciously and her blue eyes glittered with hostility. 'Roberto knew what I wanted to do—we talked about it when we met in London. I'm so glad he came through with the idea of meeting you and taking you away for a night. I think you're going to find it difficult to talk your way out of it this time. Aubrey isn't going to believe a word you say. Now, please excuse me.'

Guests arrived. The places at the tables filled up. Jeremy Jenson, tall and distinguished-looking, his white hair gleaming and contrasting with the tan he had acquired while he had been wintering at his estate in the Bahamas, came in with his wife Brenda, also tall and rather willowy, her grey hair elegantly coiffured for the occasion even if her loosely fitting flowered dress was rather drab and dowdy in comparison with the elegant clothes worn by the Italian women in the room. Aubrey was with the Jensons and so were Giovanni Palmieri and his wife from Milan. They all took their places at the table on the raised dais where Melinda and Roberto, in grey suit, white shirt and dark tie, joined them.

Giovanni welcomed everyone, first in Italian and then in English, and introduced the people at

the table with him to the guests. Jeremy received
a round of polite applause and so did Roberto.
The food was served, and Norma took her seat at
a table at the back of the room, where she could
keep an eye on the proceedings and be available
to deal with any problems that arose.

Everything went according to plan; food was
eaten, speeches were made, the signing of the
contract for making the film of *War in the Sun*
was announced and greeted with much applause,
and Jeremy signed many books. The guests
departed, and all that was left for Norma to do
was to make sure the books that hadn't been
taken by guests were packed up ready to be
dispatched to Florence, that everyone in the
kitchen was thanked and that preparations were
made for the journey to Florence the next day.
After that she would write up a report on the
whole affair in Rome for her boss at Bright &
Stevens.

'Roberto has invited us all to the Cinema City
at E.U.R. this afternoon to show us the studios
where he'll be making the film,' said Melinda,
coming over to the table where Norma was
helping to pack books into boxes. 'Are you
coming with us?'

'No. I don't have time,' said Norma shortly. 'I
have to do some paper work.'

'Okay, I'll tell him,' said Melinda serenely.
'Perhaps we'll see you later, for dinner. There's
some talk of us going to Alfredo's ... for the
publicity, of course, and the photographs with
the heaps of *fettuccine*. I'm sure I could wangle
an invitation for you.'

'No, thanks,' replied Norma coolly. 'I'd like to

turn in early. We have to be up early to catch that train to Florence, don't forget.'

She made sure she wasn't in the ballroom when Aubrey and the others left. Melinda had made it very clear that she wasn't wanted on the trip to E.U.R. or at the dinner that night. After all, she was only the hired help and not a member of the publishing, author, film-maker party, she thought wryly, even if she was engaged to be married to the managing director of the publishing company.

In her room at the desk, she chewed the end of her pen and regarded the engagement ring Aubrey had given her. She would return it to him as soon as she could get a minute alone with him. It would be best to do that before he broke the engagement. As for Roberto . . . she didn't want to think about him, because it hurt too much, hurt terribly, to think that he had met her yesterday and had taken her away with him for the afternoon and the night only to please Melinda, to help the woman convince Aubrey that he was being cheated by his fiancée. She had hoped he had met her and had taken her away because he really loved her.

She managed to get through the rest of the day without seeing any of the others and wasn't really surprised when she didn't receive any phone call from Aubrey asking her to dinner at Alfredo's. Melinda would have told him that she didn't want to go and would have made sure that he respected her decision.

She was lying in bed waiting and hoping for sleep to come when the phone rang. She let it ring three times, hoping that whoever was calling would decide either that she wasn't in the room or was asleep and would ring off. But when it rang five and then six times she gave in and picked up the receiver and switched on the bedside lamp. The fingers on her watch pointed to one o'clock.

'Yes, Norma Seton here,' she said, trying to sound as sleepy as she could.

'Why didn't you come to E.U.R. this afternoon? Why weren't you at Alfredo's?' Roberto's deep voice purred in her ear, as close as if he had been in the bed beside her. She sat up.

'I had work to do,' she replied coldly. 'And I wasn't invited to Alfredo's for dinner.'

'I invited you—through Melinda. I hoped to see you at Cinècitta to press the invitation. The dinner at Alfredo's was my party.'

She didn't say anything.

'Norma, are you still there?'

'Yes.'

'May I come up to your room? I don't have the number of it. They wouldn't give it to me at the desk, so I had to phone and ask them to put me through to you.'

'No. I don't want you to come. I . . . I don't want to see you any more. Goodbye!' She slammed down the receiver before he could say anything. The phone didn't ring again, and eventually she turned off the light and burying her face in the pillow burst into tears and sobbed as if her heart was breaking, weeping as she hadn't wept since she had been a child.

During the next three days, as they travelled to Florence, held a very successful luncheon and

ook signing there and went on to Milan with a
peat of the success, Norma had no opportunity
be alone with Aubrey to discuss the matter of
eir engagement. Melinda saw to that. And he
ade no effort to seek her out or to speak to her
rectly, making it very clear that she had earned
s disapproval.

But after the luncheon in Milan was over and
e Jensons had departed for the Bahamas Norma
ade a determined effort to get Aubrey to herself
r an hour without Melinda being present by
oning his room and inviting him to have a
ink in the bar just off the foyer of the hotel
here she had agreed to become engaged to him
November.

'We don't seem to have had a minute together
talk,' she said.

'I ... I'm not sure that I have time now,
orma. Couldn't it wait until we get back to
ondon?' he muttered.

'No, it can't be put off any longer. I know
u're annoyed with me and I think we should
scuss why you are. I can't go on like this.'

'Like what?'

'I can't go on knowing about you and Melinda,
out your affair with her, and continue to be
gaged to you.'

'I'll be in the bar in a few minutes,' he said
ickly, as she had guessed he would when she
entioned Melinda.

She was sitting at the same table at which they
d sat the last time when he came into the room.
is usually bland face was creased with worry
es, making him look his age, and his eyes
thered this way and that as if he were making

sure there was no one in the bar who knew him
making sure, perhaps, that Melinda wasn't there
He came across and sat down opposite her
looking so guilty she could have laughed out
loud.

'Now what is all this about?' he demanded.

'I'm breaking our engagement,' said Norma
and slipping off the opal ring she put it down on
the table in front of him. 'I've found out all about
you and Melinda and I've decided I can't
possibly marry a man who already has a mistress.'

His face flushing an ugly red colour, Aubrey
stared at the ring, but didn't say anything
because the waiter had come to take their order
Norma chose a Campari, Aubrey ordered his
usual gin and tonic, and the waiter went away.

'Who told you about Melinda and me?' asked
Aubrey at last in a hoarse voice.

'Roberto did, when I met him in Rome. It was
all arranged between him and her. You know, I
really thought you were going to meet me at the
airport that day I arrived, but Melinda told you
that I wouldn't be coming until the next day, and
Roberto met me and took me away so that she
could have you to herself for a few hours
They're both very good at intrigue and at stage
managing. Melinda was hoping that when you
knew I'd been with Roberto again you'd be
convinced that . . . that he and I were having a
secret affair and that I was cheating you by being
engaged to you, just as you had cheated me by
asking me to marry you when you're in love with
her. Cheated her, too.'

The waiter came with their drinks. Aubrey
seized his glass and took a good swig at it. Setting

the glass down with a click, he glared at her across the table.

'You did cheat,' he accused. 'You should have told me about your affair with Cortelli when I asked you to marry me. Why didn't you?'

'Because it was over. Because I believed it didn't matter what you or I had done before we became engaged as long as we didn't continue to meet our previous lovers once we were married; as long as we were faithful to each other after we had taken our vows.'

'You deliberately kept me in the dark about your meetings with him in Rome and Florence,' he went on, working himself up into righteous anger.

'Well, what about you?' she retorted. 'You kept me in the dark not only about Melinda but also about Lucy, your first wife. You're more of a cheat than I am. In fact I think Melinda is the only honest one among the four of us—and I can't understand why you asked me to marry you when you could marry her.'

He was silent, pushing at the ring with his forefinger, frowning at it.

'You can't do this to me, Norma. I can't let you do this after the announcements in all the papers, and the acceptance of you by my family. You can't jilt me!'

'I can and I have,' she replied, rising to her feet. 'I'm going now, to the airport. I'm leaving on an earlier flight than you and Melinda. Goodbye, Aubrey.'

'Norma, wait . . .!'

'No. Melinda is just coming in. I'm sure she'll be delighted to have a drink with you and to hear that you're not going to marry me,' she said.

She passed Melinda in the wide doorway.

'I'm off now,' she said, and held up her left hand, wiggling her fingers. 'Look, I'm free again. I'm sure you're pleased.'

'Very pleased,' said Melinda with her most brilliant smile, and walked on towards Aubrey.

Naturally when Norma returned to Bright & Stevens' offices the next day remarks were made about the absence of the opal ring from her finger, and she spent a lot of time telling everyone that her engagement to Aubrey was off, explaining that he and she were not compatible.

'Which is true enough,' Roy remarked later in the week when she told him what she had done. 'I must say I'm very relieved. I wasn't looking forward to having Aubrey as a stepson-in-law, if there is such a relationship. He's much too pernickety for me. Bit of a hypocrite too, when you think of it, pretending to be so damned prim and proper and respectable and all the time carrying on in secret with that ... what's her name?'

'Melinda.'

'Mmm. Well, it's easy to see now that he was only going to marry you to cover up his relationship with her, to hide it from his family and business associates, perhaps, to protect his reputation. You're well out of it, Norma, and I'm glad you had the guts to break off the engagement. If you'd gone ahead and married him you'd have only created a little hell for yourself.'

'That's what I think too,' agreed Norma, thinking of Roberto saying: '*They'll go on meeting, giving each other secret pleasure, and so will you and I, sweet Norma. So will you and I.* She hadn't seen or heard of him since she had said goodbye to him over the phone and she didn't expect to, but she wished there was some way she could let him know that her engagement to Aubrey was off; some way that didn't involve her lowering the banner of her pride and writing to him directly.

'How's the biography of Maria coming?' she asked Roy as casually as she could.

'Quite well,' he replied. 'Are you still mad at Roberto Cortelli for having written those letters to her and not to you?' he asked, also casual, but giving her a sly underbrowed glance.

'I wasn't mad at him for writing them to her and not to me,' she retorted with dignity. 'I just didn't like the idea of them having been ... lovers.'

'You were jealous of Maria,' he jeered.

'I was not!'

'And they were never lovers in the proper sense of the word. The affair was never consummated.'

'I know that, but only because Mama ran away and came back to England. I read that in her diary.'

'They met again, you know,' said Roy, getting up and going over to his book-strewn, paper-scattered desk and searching through the heap. She wrote about it. I came across the entry in his diary.' He peered at the book through his reading glasses. 'Yes, the diary for ten years ago, when she was at the beginning of her success and went on that tour of the States.' He flipped over pages. 'Here it is, an entry made after a concert she gave in Los Angeles.' He came around the desk and offered the book to her. 'Read that while I go and make us some coffee. It might make you feel better. It offers some good advice too, that you should consider taking.'

Norma took the book from him and he went out of the room. She looked down at her mother's neat handwriting. How had Maria ever found time to keep a diary as well as do all the other things she had done? A wonderful, wonderful woman her mother had been, beautiful, talented, serene. No wonder Roberto had loved her.

She read in the diary:

'The concert in Los Angeles was a great success. The audience's applause was heart-warming. I felt very much at home. Afterwards Roberto Cortelli came to my dressing room. He had been at the concert. He is now working in Hollywood learning all he can to become a film director, he says.

Seeing Roberto brought back many happy memories of my time with Roberto's father, in Rome, and the long talks Roberto and I used to have about poetry, opera and love. He took me to supper after the concert, and we laughed over those letters he wrote to me. He said he hoped I had forgotten and forgiven his youthful importunity in writing them to me. I told him I had forgotten his importunity long ago but that I would never forget him or the lovely words he had written in my praise. I promised to return the letters to him one day, but I couldn't do as he asked me to do. I couldn't destroy them.

Time heals all wounds eventually, making forgiveness possible. But to forget something beautiful that has given one so much pleasure is impossible. Roberto's youthful love and worship, his letters, sustained me at a time when I needed such support; when I was far away from my beloved little girl and had lost Alan, her father. So I will never forget Roberto.'

Norma closed the diary carefully and sat looking at it for a long time, and when she left Roy's house that evening to return to her flat her mother's last words on that page seemed to be branded on her mind. *I will never forget Roberto.*

February gave way to a wild and windy March. Norma trekked to and from the office at Bright & Stevens, but her heart wasn't in her work any more. She longed for change. But most of all she longed for Roberto—constantly. She longed to hear news of him. She longed to see him.

Day after day she struggled with her pride. What her mother had written had been right, she was discovering. Time did heal wounds, and she had forgiven Roberto for what he had done the last time they had met. She had forgiven him for meeting her at the airport in Rome and carrying her off to the coast just to give Melinda an opportunity to convince Aubrey that his fiancée was a cheat.

But she hadn't forgotten Roberto, and she never would.

What use was it expecting to hear from him or see him? She had told him that she didn't want to see him any more, so it was up to her to make the next move, wasn't it? To go and see him in Rome, if he was there, and to tell him . . . what? Tell him that she was willing to give up her career and live with him because she loved him and couldn't live without him?

What a confession for someone like herself to make! To admit that a man had become more important to her than her work, her freedom, her independence. How could she ever humble herself sufficiently to go to him and tell him she wanted to do as he had asked her, in November at San Gimignano; she wanted to live with him in Rome for as long as it pleased both of them. Her dilemma caused her many sleepless hours in the night.

April came in with soft mild air and flowers. Easter drew close, and the day on which she should have married Aubrey. On a sudden impulse, three days before Good Friday Norma phoned Brenton & Humbolt's offices and asked to speak to Melinda Morrison.

'How nice of you to phone,' Melinda greeted her pleasantly. 'I've been thinking about you lately, wondering what you were doing.'

'I've had a film developed at last,' said Norma. 'There are some snaps of you, quite good ones too. One by the Trevi Fountain throwing your coin in and another coming down the Spanish Steps, and another of you looking down at the ruins of the Roman Forum. I wondered if you'd like to see them. Or should I send you some prints?'

'I'd like to see them. Why don't we meet for lunch today and you can show them to me. Shall we meet by Marble Arch about twelve-thirty?'

Since it was such a lovely day they didn't go to a restaurant but bought fruit and sat on a bench in Hyde Park. Melinda liked all the snaps of

Rome and Florence that Norma had taken and asked if she could borrow the negatives so she could have some prints made.

'You can have these prints and I'll get new ones done,' said Norma generously. 'Here are some more of the first luncheon, in Rome. They've come out quite well, considering they were taken without a flash.'

Melinda studied them, holding one with herself and Roberto on it the longest.

'He's surely the most handsome man I've ever seen,' she mused. 'I suppose you know that the start of the filming of *War in the Sun* has been delayed,' she added, handing the print back to Norma.

'No, I didn't know. Why?'

'Roberto Cortelli was hurt in a skiing accident in February. He's not long out of hospital. Jeremy was over in Rome only last week to discuss the writing of the script.'

Trees, people, everything seemed to be swinging about in front of Norma. The apple she had been eating dropped from her hand. The photographic prints slipped off her knees.

Roberto hurt, his beautiful body damaged, maybe his legs, his arms broken, his head concussed!

'Oh, tell me, tell me!' she cried, turning to Melinda. 'What happened to him? How badly was he hurt? Tell me!'

'My God!' exclaimed Melinda, rolling her eyes. 'You really do get emotional, don't you? I suppose that's because you're a little bit Latin. And I just don't understand you. If you're so crazy about him what are you doing here in

London? Why didn't you stay with him in Rome the first time? Why not stay with him and live with him?'

'I . . . had to come back to my job,' muttered Norma, bending to pick up the prints. 'And then he did something I didn't like.'

'Such as?'

'That trick he played on me when he met me at Rome airport and made me go away with him. He only did it to help you to convince Aubrey I wasn't a suitable person to be his wife.'

'Oh, my God!' groaned Melinda. 'Have you been holding that against him? You are a fool! Do you really think he would have gone to meet you and taken you away if he hadn't wanted to? If he hadn't wanted to have you to himself for a few hours? Believe me, the Roberto Cortellis of this world don't do anything they don't want to do. It was his idea, remember? I didn't ask him to meet you. He suggested it, and I went along with it because it suited me too. It was my chance to see Aubrey alone and to get him back.' Melinda groaned again. 'Oh, you little fool, you little fool,' she said again. 'To hold it against him!'

'I . . . I told him I didn't want to see him any more,' muttered Norma, then, her voice rising again, 'Oh, please will you tell me how badly hurt he is, Melinda?'

'I can't, because I don't know much about the accident. But if you really care about him and want to see him again you'll go to him, tomorrow if you can, as soon as possible . . .'

'But I have to go to work tomorrow,' Norma interrupted.

'Have to? Have to?' Melinda laughed scornfully. 'Since when did a woman *have* to do anything she didn't want to do, especially when the most important man in her life is hurt and is maybe in need of her support and strength? Really, Norma, you don't know much about love, do you?'

'I'm learning—oh, I'm learning very fast,' admitted Norma ruefully. 'But do you have any other news—about you? About Aubrey?'

'We're going to get married on May the first, without his mother or his sisters being there.' Melinda made a grimce. 'But they'll come round, I know they will, when they realise what a good wife Aubrey has in me. They'll come round. And if they don't they'll lose him.'

'I'm very glad,' said Norma. 'I hope you'll both be very happy.'

'We shall,' said Melinda determinedly. 'But it wouldn't have happened if I hadn't fought for myself and found ways of disentangling him from his engagement to you. If you hadn't broken it off he would have done, you know. He was hopping mad when he found out about you and Roberto and realised you weren't the prim and proper young woman he'd assumed you to be who would make a suitable compliant wife and turn a blind eye to any extra-marital affair he might have with me. Thank God you met Roberto when you did, and that I met him too. He's a wonderful person, Norma. and if you've any sense you'll be on the next flight to Rome to see him.'

Norma wasn't able to get a reservation on a flight to Rome until the afternoon of the following day,

Wednesday. After making the reservation she asked Bill Graham, her boss, if she could have Wednesday and Thursday off to attend to some personal business. He wasn't at all co-operative and refused.

'You'll have all Friday, Saturday, Sunday and next Monday. Plenty of time to attend to personal problems,' he said.

So there was nothing else for her to do but take French leave on Wednesday and Thursday and hope that she didn't lose her job as a result. She wasn't able to tell Roy she was going to Rome because he had already gone away to some conference of university professors.

As the plane took off on Wednesday afternoon and she looked down at the gleaming river, the Houses of Parliament and the Tower of London, she had a strange feeling that she had burned her boats and that it would be a long time before she returned to London.

CHAPTER TEN

At Rome airport, after de-planing and going through the usual preliminaries of Immigration and Customs, Norma dithered. Should she phone the house on the Via Scipione and make sure Roberto was there, announce her arrival and ask if she could visit him? Or should she just go and arrive unannounced and risk being turned away at his gate by the impassive and somehow disapproving Paolo?

While she hesitated she went to the currency exchange and changed some pound notes into the usual numerous *lire*. As she turned away from the counter she was approached by a handsome young man who told her in excellent English that he was the information officer of the airport and asked if he could help her.

'Where are you going, *signorina*?' he asked.

'Oh . . . to a house on the Via Scipione. I know where it is, but . . .'

'Then you will need a taxi,' he interrupted her authoritatively, and waved a hand to some men who were lingering near the exit doors. One of them came over, and the information officer spoke to him rapidly in Italian, then turned back to Norma with his scintillating Italian charm.

'This driver knows the street you want. You have the number of the house, *signorina*? It is important for him to know it because many of the streets are one-way and he wishes to enter it at the right end.'

She gave him the number of the Cortelli house, and so it was taken out of her hands by the two charmingly authoritative men who obviously were quite convinced that no woman could fend for herself in Rome without their help, and she was whisked out to the waiting yellow Fiat that was the taxi, her luggage was put in the boot and the car sped away from the airport.

It was lovely to be back, thought Norma as she sat looking out at the fields all freshly green now under the afternoon sunshine. It felt right to be there, and when they reached Rome itself and she had glimpses of familiar buildings and towers and domes of old churches, the columns of Romanesque structures, the plane trees beside the river, their leaves a delicate new green, the pines, the unforgettable umbrella pines, she realised how much she had wanted to come back during the past few weeks; how much she had been pining not just for Roberto, but for this city where she had felt so much at home.

At last they crossed the bridge near the Via Scipione, which they shared with a Metro train going the other way. Into the street with its elegant old buildings, trees and courtyards they turned, and stopped outside the wrought iron gates set in the golden-brown walls of the Cortelli house.

The driver of the taxi took her case out of the boot. Norma gave him what seemed to her an enormous number of *lire* and he drove away. Picking up her case, she approached the gate and pressed the bell-push.

Her heart was racing with excitement. Soon she would see Roberto. How would he look after being in an accident? Oh, she did hope he hadn't been injured too badly. Suppose he wouldn't see her, what would she do? Die on the spot, probably like some lovelorn heroine in an old Italian romance. Die as Juliet had died when she had seen her Romeo lying dead. Die as Isabella had died pining for her Lorenzo. She gave herself a little shake. Of course she wouldn't die if Roberto spurned her, but she would suffer just the same. She would suffer a living death.

The front door of the house opened. Paolo, his white jacket crisp and stark, came along the path, and stared at her with unwinking opaque eyes. She told him she had come to see Signor Cortelli and gave her name. He inclined his head without a word and to her great relief unlocked the gate and led her into the courtyard.

The green shrubs were thick, their leaves shiny as if they had just been polished. Tiny pale pink petals fell from an almond tree in blossom. The entrance hall was silent and sunlit, the living room shabbily elegant as ever. Paolo indicated that she should leave her case just by the open French window and pointed to the patio. His back to her, Roberto was lounging on one of the garden chairs. Sitting near to him, reading something from a sheaf of papers, was a girl with long black hair.

Paolo suggested to Norma that she went outside, but she asked him to go first and announce her. He gave her a rather impatient glance and moved ahead of her to go down the steps to the patio, stepping awkwardly as if his legs were very stiff, and she realised suddenly why he didn't want to go. He had arthritis and disliked going up or down steps or stairs.

'It's all right,' she said quickly, 'I'll announce myself.'

At the sound of her voice Roberto turned his head quickly. Across the space of a few yards he stared at her and she stared back at him. The young woman with the black hair stopped reading and turned to stare at Norma, then looked back at Roberto. Paolo went back into the house.

'I . . . I happened to be in Rome, so I thought I'd call to see you,' said Norma, going down the steps. The fountain tinkled, the air was warm and full of the scents of shrubs and flowers. The patio was a place of secret beauty and tranquillity, walled off from the noise and dirt of city traffic, an oasis of peace. 'I . . . I'd heard you'd had an accident.'

As always the sight of him, black hair springing back from his forehead, classically sculptured face calm and composed, long dark eyes regarding her with that slight smile in them as if he knew much about her that she didn't know herself, knocked all the breath out of her. Her legs shook and before he could stand up she sat down abruptly on the nearest chair.

'I did—I broke my left leg in two places. Stupid of me,' he replied coolly. 'But it's out of the cast now and I'm walking quite well.' He glanced past her at the other girl. 'Adrianna, I'd like you to meet Norma Seton,' he said. 'Norma, this is Adrianna Roscetti, from New York.'

'Pleased to meet you, Norma,' said the

American girl. She was about twenty years of age, had a creamy complexion, large dark eyes, a mane of silky black hair and full red lips that curved back from perfect teeth. Her curvaceous figure was set off to advantage in a tight-fitting shirt that was unbuttoned to the cleft between her full breasts.

'How do you do?' said Norma rather primly, trying to hide the fact that she was taken aback by the presence of the other girl and feeling a twinge of jealousy of her because she was here in this secret place with Roberto.

'Oh, you're English!' exclaimed Adrianna, opening her eyes wide.

'Norma is a little bit Italian,' said Roberto. 'Her mother was Maria Crossley, an opera singer.'

'Really?' Adrianna looked interested in an ingenuous youthful way. 'Like Grandpapa. Do you sing too?'

'No . . . I'm in business,' answered Norma. She couldn't help feeling disappointed. She had looked forward all day to this meeting with Roberto and now that she was here everything was different from what she had expected. He wasn't suffering and in great pain or in need of womanly comfort. He looked actually very well and had already acquired a tan which was set off by the white shirt he was wearing. He wasn't in any obvious pain, and worst of all, he had this young and vitally beautiful girl with him.

'Is that why you are in Rome?' asked Roberto casually. 'On business?'

'I . . . er . . . no. I'm on holiday—for Easter, you know,' she told him.

'But I thought. . . .' He broke off and turned to Adrianna with a touch of irritation in his manner. 'Go and ask Paolo to mix us some drinks and you bring them out to us to save him the trip,' he ordered. 'Campari for Norma, Scotch on the rocks for me and you please yourself what you have. And bring some roasted almonds.'

'Okay. Whatever you say, boss,' retorted Adrianna, springing to her feet. She gave him the sheaf of papers from which she had been reading and walked towards the house. Norma watched her go, thinking how sexily Adrianna moved and wondering uneasily if the young woman was living with Roberto, sleeping with him, sharing his life. Her hands clenched convulsively on her handbag which lay on her knees. Perhaps she had come too late. Oh God, what would she do if she had? What was she going to do?

She turned to look at him. He was watching her, his face composed, his eyes watchful.

'She's . . . she's very pretty,' she mumbled.

'She's more than that. She's beautiful,' he replied.

'Has she been here . . . in Rome . . . long?'

'Since the middle of February. She was with me when I fell on the slopes at Aosta.'

'I'm sorry you were hurt.'

'Who told you?' he asked.

'Melinda.'

'Ah, yes, of course. She would have heard from Jenson. The accident delayed the work on the script for the film and meant he had to come here to Rome to write it with me instead of me going to the Bahamas as we had arranged. But it's finished now.' He pointed to the sheaf of paper now lying on the small patio table and gave her a humorously glinting glance. 'Like to try for a part, while you're here? Adrianna is. She has great potential to be a sultry beauty of the silver screen and is a natural when it comes to acting.'

'No, thank you,' she replied. 'I . . . I won't wait for a drink thank you.' She stood up. 'I just thought I'd call in and. . . .'

'Sit down!' Roberto rapped the words at her and leaned forward as if he was threatening to push her back on to the chair.

'I really should go . . .'

'Where? Where will you go?' he demanded, glaring up at her. 'To Aubrey? Is he waiting in some hotel for you? Have you been married already and have come here on your honeymoon?' His upper lip curled in a sneer. 'I'd have thought you'd have had more taste than to have chosen Rome for it after your affair here with me!'

'No, no! I'm not married to Aubrey and he isn't here waiting for me. I came on my own.'

'Then you have time to sit down, time to stay for dinner, time for . . .'

'No, I haven't—really. I have to find a hotel to stay in.'

'You can stay here. Now sit down and tell me why you're not married to Aubrey. Who broke it off? Did he?'

Slowly Norma sank down on to the chair again. A movement at the french window drew her attention. Adrianna was coming out, walking cautiously as she carried a small tray on which there were two glasses and a small dish.

'Here are your drinks, oh, lord and master,' Adrianna said facetiously as she set the tray down on the table. 'I'm not having one—I'm going to shower and change. See you later. You too, Norma, I hope.' She smiled at Norma and then with a swirl of her long black hair went back into the house.

Leaning forward, Roberto picked up the tall glass of Campari and handed it to Norma. She took it from him. Ice cubes clinked in it. He picked up his Scotch and helping himself to a handful of the roasted almonds leaned back in his chair. She noticed he sat with his left leg stretched before him and that a walking stick hung over the back of his chair.

'About Aubrey,' he said, crunching nuts between his teeth. 'Did he jilt you after he discovered you'd been with me?'

'No.' She sipped some of her drink. 'I broke off the engagement, in Milan, after the last luncheon party.'

'You did?' His eyebrows went up. 'Why?'

'I decided I didn't want to be married to him after I'd found out that he was only marrying me to cover up his affair with Melinda,' she muttered.

'So you believed what I told you about them?'

'After Melinda had told me of the arrangement she made with you to meet me at the airport that day and take me away for the night so she could convince Aubrey that I was ... was—well, she accused me of cheating him.'

'And weren't you?' he drawled, not looking at her but at his drink, his eyes hidden by the fringes of his lashes.

'Not as much as he was going to cheat me. At least my affair with you was over. I wasn't going to see you any more, not after I'd married him.'

He looked up quickly, his eyes narrowed, searching her face.

'That was the last thing you said to me,' he remarked. 'You were very angry. I could hear your anger sizzling over the telephone wire.' He grinned. 'I couldn't understand why you were mad at me.'

'Oh, it was because you . . . you'd come to meet me and taken me away to Sorino to please Melinda, so that she could have some time with Aubrey, so that she could convince him I wasn't a suitable person for him to marry,' Norma said hotly, recalling her anger with him. 'You . . . you deceived me. That's why I didn't want to see you any more.'

'I didn't intend to deceive you and I still don't think I did. I went to meet you to please myself, not Melinda. I presented her with an opportunity to use to her advantage, which I'm sure she did.' He leaned towards her and looked into her eyes. 'I came to meet you because I wanted to see you again and I wanted to have you to myself for a few hours, and after your initial "passive resistance" you seemed glad that I'd met you and had taken you to Sorino.' His lips twisted again. 'Or was that just an act you were putting on, a way of getting some physical satisfaction while you could, using me, because I happened to be available, to get your kicks?'

'Oh!' Outraged by his insinuation that she was the sort of woman who slept around, Norma saw red for a few seconds—and during those few seconds she threw the contents of her glass right in his face. Then, horrified at what she had done, while he was still spluttering and wiping Campari off his face, she sprang to her feet, put the glass down on the tray and made for the french window.

'Oh, no you don't, you little hellion, you spitfire, you!' Amazingly Roberto was out of his chair and had limped after her. Grabbing her arm, he swung her around to face him as if she were a doll made from straw so that her head swung on her neck. When everything stopped jigging around she was able to see his face. He looked ready to commit murder, his eyes stormy, his lips snarling. 'You don't do that to me and get away with it,' he muttered in a vicious whisper. 'You're going to pay for that!'

'Well, I couldn't let you say what you did about me and get away with it,' she raged. 'I didn't sleep with you, make love with you in Sorino, just to . . . just because I wanted a man,' she went on in a lower voice. 'I'm not like that. I've never been like that, and I've never done what I did with you with any other man.'

'Then why with me, Norma?' he said softly, the murderous expression fading, his eyes growing dark with tenderness, his grip on her arm losing its bite but not relaxing, his other hand coming up to take hold of her other arm so that he could draw her towards him. 'Why with me?'

'Hey, you two, I hate to interrupt,' Adrianna spoke from the open window, 'but Paolo wants to know how many for dinner tonight.'

'Two,' said Roberto, not turning his head to look at Adrianna, but continuing to look at Norma. 'Norma will be staying to dinner and you will be going out.'

'Oh. Okay, whatever you say, sir,' Adrianna quipped jauntily, and disappeared into the room.

'No, I'm not staying,' said Norma. 'I . . . I have to go. Please, Roberto, let me go. Let me go!' she tried to twist free, but his hands tightened on her arms and he hauled her against him.

'No, never,' he whispered, his lips almost touching hers. 'Not again. You've come to me this time of your own accord and there's no Aubrey for you to run away to any more. You're here to stay.'

'You can't make me stay,' she argued, but her heart wasn't in the argument.

'I know a very good way of persuading you,' he taunted.

'But . . . but what about Adrianna? You're not . . . surely you're not going to turn her out?' She put her hands on his chest in an attempt to push him away from her. 'Oh, you're despicable when it comes to women! Hardly had you finished with me when you took up with her, and . . . and now that I've come back you're going to give her the push. Or are you going to juggle the two of us . . .'

'Shut up!' he hissed, his lips thinning, his eyes blazing again. 'Stop insulting me!'

'You insult me, so why shouldn't I insult you? Anyway, I'm only telling the truth, and you said once to me that the truth always hurts . . . oh, now what are you doing?'

He had taken hold of one of her wrists and was pulling her after him towards the french window. Up the steps he limped, and she had to go with him because she couldn't pull free. Inside the room he shouted,

'Adrianna? Adrianna?' and marched towards the doorway out into the entrance hall. Halfway up the stairs Adrianna paused and looked down at them. Norma tried to look as if she hadn't been dragged into the hallway, all the time trying to wriggle her wrist out of Roberto's grip.

'Yes?' the dark-haired girl queried uncertainly.

'Get down here,' ordered Roberto.

'Now what have I done?' demanded Adrianna rather sulkily, but she came, just the same, slowly, moving with indolent sexy movements of her curved hips and staring at Roberto insolently.

'You haven't done anything except to be here this afternoon,' Roberto growled at her. 'Now tell Norma who you are.'

'But you've already introduced me,' complained Adrianna, plonking down on to the last stair and staying there. 'What's with you, Uncle Roberto? You going through the change early or something?'

'Tell Norma who you are, what your relationship is to me.'

'Oh.' Adrianna's sunny smile appeared. 'I get you—although she should have guessed by now, because I just called you Uncle. I'm his niece. My mother is his elder sister.' She glanced from Norma back to Roberto and then back again to Norma, her big brown eyes curious. 'Why, what did you think . . . oh, no!' she started to laugh. 'You didn't think I was his latest lover, did you? Oh, gosh, how funny!' She sobered as suddenly as she had started to laugh. 'It's your own fault, Uncle Roberto. You should have told Norma who I am when you introduced me if you didn't want her to get the wrong idea.' She looked at Norma again. 'If you're really interested, he hasn't been seeing anyone else all the time I've been here. In fact he's been terribly anti-social. Most unlike him, Mom says. Do you mind if I go and have my shower now? I have a date in exactly half an hour.'

'Who is it this time?' enquired Roberto mockingly. 'The bartender from the hotel down the street? Or the mailman?'

'Neither.' Adrianna stuck her tongue out at him disrespectfully and took the stairs two at a time.

Norma was at last able to free her wrist from the vicelike grip in which it had been caught. Rubbing it ostentatiously, she said accusingly,

'You deliberately didn't introduce her to me as your niece. You wanted me to think she was your latest . . . lover, didn't you?'

'Perhaps.'

She looked up at him. Hands in his trouser pockets, he was looking at her, his eyes dark and brooding.

'I'm sorry I said what I did to you about making love with me because I happened to be available,' he said stiffly. 'It wasn't hard to believe that of you after you had told me you didn't want to see me any more.'

'I'm sorry I threw my Campari at you. You . . . you make me so angry that . . . that I don't know what I'm doing or saying.' She paused, still rubbing at her wrist, looking at her fingers moving around it, then burst out, 'Oh, perhaps it would be best if we didn't see each other any more, if we didn't meet again. We only hurt each other when we're together. Please let me go, Roberto. Please open the gate and let me out.'

'No.'

'Why not?' She raised her head again to look at him, not bothering to hide the tears that had sprung to her eyes at the thought of having to part from him again.

'I'll tell you if you'll tell me why you did what you did with me here, in Florence and in Sorino, what you've never done with any other man,' he said quietly. 'Why me, Norma?'

'Oh, it isn't fair!' she cried. 'Why should I give in first? Why not you? Why won't you tell me why you won't let me leave this house, why you want me to stay to dinner?'

'I won't let you leave, and I want you to stay to dinner because I want to make love to you,' he said simply. 'I want you to stay and live with me for the same reason I asked you to come back here and live with me when we were in San Gimignano. I love you and I want you. Now it's your turn, Norma. Tell me, why did you choose to do it with me?'

There was no way she could avoid telling him now. He had said more than she had ever expected him to say.

'Oh, I . . . I chose you because I love you,' she confessed, and didn't resist him at all when he swept her into his arms to kiss her hungrily.

And so she stayed to dinner and stayed the night, sharing with him the wide bed in the big bedroom that they had shared one night in November, and their lovemaking was all the more pleasurable because no longer was there any strain between them, no suspicion by either of the other's motives. Their bodies and souls were joined in perfect union, and next morning they were more at ease in each other's company than they had ever been.

'So you're the one Uncle Roberto has been yearning for these past weeks,' Adrianna said in her frank way when Norma met her at breakfast. Roberto had gone out early to audition some actors and actresses who had applied for roles in his new film.

'Has he been yearning?' asked Norma as she broke a hot fresh roll and began to butter it.

'As near to it as a man like him would ever get,' said Adrianna. 'He was a real grouch when Mom and I arrived at the end of February, and Mom recognised the signs. She said he hadn't been able to get something he wanted. And he wasn't much fun in Aosta. I don't think he would have broken his leg if his mind had been on what he was doing—skiing—and not on you.'

'Oh, now you're making me feel responsible for the accident,' groaned Norma.

'Sorry,' said Adrianna brightly. 'Are you going to live with him, here in this house?'

'I . . . I'm not sure,' Norma replied. It was the truth; she wasn't sure. Although yesterday when she had arrived Roberto had asked her to stay and live with him, and although he had confessed he loved her, she still felt he hadn't committed himself to her. He was still holding back a part of himself and so making it difficult for her to make a commitment to him.

'I'm going to the Villa Borghese Park this morning,' announced Adrianna. 'Roberto says I must see the museum. There wasn't time to go

when Mom was here. She had to fly back to
Rome to go to some convention with Pops. He'
in business . . . financial investment. Mom let me
stay on here with Roberto because he said he'd
like me to take a screen test for a role in *War in
the Sun*. I'm so excited about it! Who knows,
might became an *instant* film star!' Adrianna
preened herself, then laughed at herself endear
ingly and added, 'Anyway, would you like to
come to the Borghese Gallery with me?'

'Yes, I would.'

'Great. And afterwards we could have lunch
together—I know a good little place in the Vi
della Croce, near Spanish Square. And afterward
we could go shopping. You'll get awfull
lonesome if you don't come, hanging about
waiting for Roberto to come back. He'll be a
Cinema City for hours and hours. Once he get
involved in film-making, he forgets everything
and everyone else, Mom says. I guess he isn't th
stuff from which good husbands are made, bu
then creative people rarely are. Don't you agree?

Each room in the Borghese Gallery was a work o
art with intricately decorated walls and ceilings
There was so much to stand and stare at tha
Norma and Adrianna were there until the museun
closed at two o'clock, admiring the graceful statue
of Apollo and Daphne and also the biblical Davi
by Bernini, as well as the wonderfully likelik
sculpture of Pauline Bonaparte Borghese b
Canova. There were also many superb paintings b
Raphael, Caravaggio and Titian, and Norma tol
Adrianna about the painting of an unknown mar
she had seen in the Uffizi Gallery in Florence wh
she had thought had looked like Roberto.

'Roberto is handsome, isn't he?' agreed Adrianna as they left the museum and stepped out into the warm spring sunshine to wander along the pathway to the Via Pinciano where they intended to catch a bus. 'Mom always says that being so good-looking hasn't done him much good. He's always attracted women he hasn't wanted or who have spoiled him dreadfully. I should think that one reason why he likes you is because you're cool and just a little offhand, not always available and not always gushing over him.'

Surprised by Adrianna's insight—she had discovered that the girl wasn't as old as she looked but was barely eighteen—Norma found a certain comfort in learning that she had attracted Roberto because she was a little different from the other women he had known.

But how long would that attraction last? Wouldn't it wear off if she stayed and lived with him in Rome? If she became his mistress and was available all the time wouldn't he lose interest in her eventually?

'He doesn't seem much interested in marriage,' she remarked casually to Adrianna.

'Oh, I guess that's because of the bad example set by Grandpop Cortelli and Grandmama,' replied Adrianna. 'They always fought when they were together, Mom says. Not that Grandpops was at home much. They were two tough characters, it seems. Neither would give in to the other. It seems that compromise was something neither of them understood. Both of them were too artistic, I guess. Grandmama is a painter. She's not bad, either. She was part of the

Abstract Expressionist movement in the States
She knew some really big names—Jackson
Pollock, de Cooney, that crowd.'

'Oh,' said Norma, who hadn't heard o
Abstract Expressionism and didn't recognise the
names of the artists Adrianna had mentioned.

'That's another reason why Grandmama
wouldn't move away from Long Island when
Grandpops wanted to come back to Rome. She
wanted to stay where she could go on creating
she said. She didn't think she could do it in
Rome. And Grandpops said he couldn't teach
singing anywhere else. So they split,' Adrianna
added. 'Oh, here's our bus at last.'

Later when she returned to the house on the
Via Scipione after first lunching with Adrianna
and then shopping with her, Norma had to admit
that the day would have seemed very long if she
had had to spend it alone. As it was, the evening
dragged as she tried to amuse herself. Adrianna
had gone out on a date and Roberto didn't return
for dinner, nor did he phone. The TV programmes were boring and there was no one to
talk to.

It would be like this if she came to live with
him, she thought, as she prepared for bed. She
would spend hours wondering when he would
return or if he would return. She would become
consumed by jealousy, imagining he was enjoying
himself with some of the women who acted in his
films. Only if she had something to do; only if
she had a career of her own to follow would she
be able to live here with him.

She was asleep when he came at last. He
woke her with kisses and then made love to her

silently and swiftly, obliterating her anxieties
about their relationship with subtle, tantalising
caresses until her body seemed to burst open
with unbearable desire, and she reached out
with both hands to pull him down on her to
take what he wanted.

Afterwards he murmured,

'How long are you going to stay?'

'I go back on Monday afternoon.'

'Why go back?' he asked, sliding a roving hand
over her waist and hips, nibbling at her ear with
sharp teeth.

'I still work for Bright & Stevens.'

'And they are more important than I am?' he
growled softly. 'They are still more important
than *us* and what we have going between us?'

'You're jealous of a company?' she teased.

'I'm jealous of anyone or anything that takes
you away from me.'

'So . . . you would understand if . . . if I tell
you I'm jealous of your film-making because it
takes you away from me?' she challenged him.

He was silent for a while, lying still, not
caressing her any more. Then he said with a
touch of bitterness,

'We seem to have a problem to solve. Let's
forget it for now. We have tomorrow, Saturday,
Sunday and most of Monday together. Is there
anywhere you would like to go? I'll be at your
command for three whole days.'

Norma turned so that she could see his face by
the light of the bedside lamp. The dark grey eyes
looked back at her, a hint of a smile in their
depths, that enigmatic smile that mocked her
even while it adored her.

'I'd like to go wherever you want to go and d
what you want to do,' she said quietly.

'That sounds almost like commitment,' h
mocked her, and blew gently at the frond of hai
on her brow. 'And I am going to take you at you
word. We'll go south again, further than las
time. Maybe to Pompeii to see the old villas tha
have been found under the ashes that wer
spewed out by Vesuvius nearly two thousan
years ago, and maybe further to the Amalfi coast
Would you like that?'

'I would love it,' she whispered, kissing him i
grateful anticipation, determined to do as h
suggested and to forget their problem for a whil
as they seized together the opportunity to escap
into a world of their own.

Three days of sunshine and blue skies the
had, another longer and more golden spell tha
the one they had known in November; a spe
during which all that mattered was being togethe
in places whose names were synonymous wit
beauty and romance.

Blue-green against the blue sky, Moun
Vesuvius dominated Pompeii, always there,
reminder of devastating destructive power beyon
the control of mankind. Glancing down a cobble
street of shops, or through an ancient archway i
the Forum, or over the columns of the peristyl
in the garden of the House of the Faun, Norm
would see the sloping walls of the mountain an
would wonder what it had been like for th
inhabitants of the ancient city when molten lav
and hot ash had swept down on them and ha
buried them alive.

There was so much to see and so little time i

hich to see it. Completely captivated by the
racious villas, the wonderful murals, the graceful
olumns and the flourishing gardens, they
romised themselves a return visit and, as the sun
egan to set, they drove on along the winding
limbing road that often seemed to hang right
ver the wine-coloured sea, to the city of
orrento, white houses, Renaissance palaces and
aroque churches, high on a clifftop above the
ay of Naples.

Another night of love, star-studded and
ccompanied by the whisper of unseen waves,
ad then an awakening to another day of perfect
eather. A drive along the Amalfi road, twisting
ad turning. White villages tumbled down cliffs
› the edge of the sea. Mountains shimmered in
ae distance, purple, green and silver. Orange and
mon groves covered the hillsides.

Never would she forget those three days,
ought Norma on Monday morning as they
rove back from Sorino where they had spent
unday night in the *pensione* they had visited in
ebruary. Never.

But once again it was nearly over, their time
›gether, their secret pleasure, and soon they
ould part at Rome airport. They sat in silence,
oth muted by sadness. At least it was sadness
aat made Norma quiet. About Roberto she was
ot so sure.

She glanced at him. Nothing to be learned
om that severely sculptured profile, and yet the
roblem was still with them, the problem they
ad both successfully forgotten for three whole
ays.

Would he bring it up for discussion before they

reached the airport? Or would he wait for her t
mention it first? She looked away from him out o
the window. Fields and trees were blurred. B
tears? No, by rain. Sunshine and blue skies ha
gone. Rain was more suitable for partings. Ol
God, what was she going to do? She couldn
bear to say goodbye to him again. She must sa
something, find out what the future held for th
two of them.

'Will you come to visit me in London?' sh
ventured.

'Not for a while. I must start making the film
make up for the time I lost through the acciden
When can you come to Rome again?' He wa
coolly practical.

'I don't know,' she whispered. Then sh
seemed to burst apart with anguish. 'Oh, I don
want to go back today! I want to stay in Rome.
want to stay with you always. Oh, what shall
do? What shall I do?'

Hands over her face, she began to so
uncontrollably. The car slowed down an
stopped. Roberto switched off the engine. Rai
drummed heavily on the roof. Turning to her, h
gathered her into his arms, held her until h
sobs had subsided. She felt his fingers in her hai
stroking her temple, then her cheek.

'But you can stay with me in Rome,' he sai
softly. 'You don't have to leave. I have alway
wanted you to stay, ever since our first meetin
But the decision has to be yours. I can't make
for you. You can stay, if you want to—for ever.

'But I'm afraid to,' she sniffled against h
shoulder.

'Why?'

'I'm afraid of being jealous of your work. I'm afraid of being restless with nothing to do all day. But most of all I'm afraid that you . . . you'll stop loving me.'

He was very quiet for a long time. The rain continued to pour. In the shelter of his arms Norma felt safe. They were walls to protect her and his strength was a tower standing sentinel over her.

'We could get married,' he said suddenly.

She pushed up and away from him so that she could see his face. He looked at her, eyes dark and secretive, measuring her.

'But I thought . . . I mean, I had the impression you don't care for marriage,' she whispered, remembering what Adrianna had told her about the effect his parents' marriage had had on him.

'I didn't have much respect for the institution until I met you,' he replied, with a cynical curl to his lip.

'Then . . . why change your mind?'

'You have changed it for me,' he replied, smiling at her. 'You see, I have this feeling that if we were married you would feel better about living with me on a more permanent basis. Am I right?'

Norma nodded her agreement, feeling hope begin to flower among the turbulence of her emotions.

'But I have to warn you, Norma, that if we got married I couldn't have you running back to London to your job all the time,' he continued rather sternly. 'You would have to live where I live, go where I go . . . like that woman in the

Bible, what was her name? Ruth? We would have to be together most of the time. You understand?'

'Yes, I think so. You wouldn't want me to be like Maria, going off around the world for eight months, or like your mother refusing to live where your father wanted to live,' she agreed.

'You put it very well,' he said dryly. 'And if you really have to go to work you could get a job here, in Rome.'

'Where?'

'With a film company I know about.' A glint in his eyes mocked her.

'Oh, now wait a minute! I'm not going to take a screen test, not even if you marry me. I'm not going to act in one of your films,' she asserted herself.

'I wasn't thinking of asking you to, again,' he retorted. 'But you could work on the promotional side, couldn't you? Don't you have a very high opinion of your own abilities when it comes to public relations?'

'You would really offer me a job in P.R.?' she whispered.

'I am offering you a job as mistress, as wife, as P.R. director for Cortelli films, whatever it is you want to do, as long as you stay with me and live with me. As long as you stop running away from me. So what is your answer? Is it yes, you'll stay? Or no, you'll go back to London and we'll never meet again?'

'Is that an ultimatum you're issuing?' Norma queried, tilting her chin.

'It is. We either stay together for always or we part right now for good.'

She studied his face. Dark and ruthless,

relentless. She knew he meant every word of the ultimatum. Staying with him she would have moments of secret pleasure, glimpses of paradise. Parting from him for good would be a heartbreak from which she might never recover.

'I'll stay ... for always, and we'll be married, and I promise I won't run away from you or from love again,' she whispered, committed at last. And suddenly it seemed as if joy and hope burst through her tears and sadness just as the sun burst through the rain clouds and lit the scene with a rainbow, and she let her love for him take over finally and for ever. 'Oh, it's a wonderful solution to our problem! I'm so glad you thought of it. Oh, Roberto, you're wonderful!' she cried, and flinging her arms around him she kissed him.

'I think I'm wonderful too,' he agreed with a mocking grin as he started the car. 'But I'm glad you brought the matter up when you did. I was doing my best to drive slowly so that you would miss that flight to London. Now I'm sure you've missed it, and you'll have to stay another night with me.'

'I'll be staying for always,' she reminded him.

'Always, then. So shall we go home now, sweet Norma, home to Rome?' he queried softly.

'Yes, let's go home to Rome,' she agreed happily.

Coming Next Month in Harlequin Presents!

839 BITTER ENCORE—Helen Bianchin
Nothing can erase the memory of their shared passion. But can an estranged couple reunite when his star status still leaves no room for her in his life—except in his bed?

840 FANTASY—Emma Darcy
On a secluded beach near Sydney, a model, disillusioned by her fiancé, finds love in the arms of a stranger. Or is it all a dream—this man, this fantasy?

841 RENT-A-BRIDE LTD—Emma Goldrick
Fearful of being forced to marry her aunt's stepson, an heiress confides in a fellow passenger on her flight from Denver—never thinking he'd pass himself off as her new husband!

842 WHO'S BEEN SLEEPING IN MY BED?—Charlotte Lamb
The good-looking playwright trying to win her affection at the family villa in France asks too many questions about her father's affairs. She's sure he's using her.

843 STOLEN SUMMER—Anne Mather
She's five years older, a friend of the family's. And he's engaged! How can she take seriously a young man's amorous advances? Then again, how can she not?

844 LIGHTNING STORM—Anne McAllister
A young widow returns to California and re-encounters the man who rejected her years before—a man after a good time with no commitments. Does lightning really strike twice?

845 IMPASSE—Margaret Pargeter
Unable to live as his mistress, a woman left the man she loves. Now he desires her more than ever—enough, at least, to ruin her engagement to another man!

846 FRANGIPANI—Anne Weale
Her sister's offer to find her a millionaire before they dock in Fiji is distressing. She isn't interested. But the captain of the ship finds that hard to believe....

H·A·R·L·E·Q·U·I·N

FIRST·CLASS
Sweepstakes

OFFICIAL RULES

1. NO PURCHASE NECESSARY. To enter, complete the official entry/order form. Be sure to indicate whether or not you wish to take advantage of our subscription offer.

2. Entry blanks have been preselected for the prizes offered. Your response will be checked to see if you are a winner. In the event that these preselected responses are not claimed, a random drawing will be held from all entries received to award not less than $150,000 in prizes. This is in addition to any free, surprise or mystery gifts which might be offered. Versions of this sweepstakes with different prizes will appear in Preview Service Mailings by Harlequin Books and their affiliates. Winners selected will receive the prize offered in their sweepstakes brochure.

3. This promotion is being conducted under the supervision of Marden-Kane, an independent judging organization. By entering the sweepstakes, each entrant accepts and agrees to be bound by these rules and the decisions of the judges, which shall be final and binding. Odds of winning in the random drawing are dependent upon the total number of entries received. Taxes, if any, are the sole responsibility of the prize winners. Prizes are nontransferable. All entries must be received by August 31, 1986.

4. The following prizes will be awarded:

   (1) Grand Prize: Rolls-Royce™ *or* $100,000 Cash!
   (Rolls-Royce being offered by permission of Rolls-Royce Motors Inc.)

   (1) Second Prize: A trip for two to Paris for 7 days/6 nights. Trip includes air transportation on the Concorde, hotel accommodations...PLUS...$5,000 spending money!

   (1) Third Prize: A luxurious Mink Coat!

5. This offer is open to residents of the U.S. and Canada, 18 years or older, except employees of Harlequin Books, its affiliates, subsidiaries, Marden-Kane and all other agencies and persons connected with conducting this sweepstakes. All Federal, State and local laws apply. Void in the province of Quebec and wherever prohibited or restricted by law. Winners will be notified by mail and may be required to execute an affidavit of eligibility and release, which must be returned within 14 days after notification. Canadian winners will be required to answer a skill-testing question. Winners consent to the use of their name, photograph and/or likeness for advertising and publicity purposes in conjunction with this and similar promotions without additional compensation. One prize per family or household.

6. For a list of our most current prize winners, send a stamped, self-addressed envelope to: WINNERS LIST, c/o Marden-Kane, P.O. Box 10404, Long Island City, New York 11101

Here's how to get this special offer from Harlequin!
As simple as 1...2...3!

NOVEMBER
TREASURY EDITION
COUPON

1. Each month, save one Treasury Edition coupon from your favorite Romance or Presents novel.
2. In four months you'll have saved four Treasury Edition coupons (<u>only one coupon per month allowed</u>).
3. Then all you have to do is fill out and return the order form provided, along with the four Treasury Edition coupons required and $1.00 for postage and handling.

Mail to: Harlequin Reader Service

RT1-D-2

In the U.S.A.
2504 West Southern Ave.
Tempe, AZ 85282

In Canada
P.O. Box 2800, Postal Station A
5170 Yonge Street
Willowdale, Ont. M2N 6J3

Please send me my FREE copy of the Janet Dailey Treasury Edition. I have enclosed the four Treasury Edition coupons required and $1.00 for postage and handling along with this order form.

(Please Print)

NAME_____

ADDRESS_____

CITY_____

STATE/PROV._____ ZIP/POSTAL CODE_____

SIGNATURE_____
This offer is limited to one order per household.

SUPPLIES LIMITED

This special Janet Dailey offer expires January 1986.